More Than Protect You

Also From Shayla Black

CONTEMPORARY ROMANCE

MORE THAN WORDS
More Than Want You
More Than Need You
More Than Love You
More Than Crave You
More Than Tempt You
More Than Pleasure You (novella)
More Than Dare You
More Than Protect You (novella)
Coming Soon:
More Than Hate You (Summer 2021)

WICKED & DEVOTED
Wicked as Sin
Wicked Ever After
Coming Soon:
Wicked as Lies (February 9, 2021)
Wicked and True (March 16, 2021)

THE WICKED LOVERS (Complete Series)
Wicked Ties
Decadent
Delicious
Surrender To Me
Belong To Me
"Wicked to Love" (novella)
Mine To Hold
"Wicked All The Way" (novella)
Ours To Love
Wicked All Night – Wicked and Dangerous Anthology
"Forever Wicked" (novella)
Theirs To Cherish
His to Take
Pure Wicked (novella)
Wicked for You

Falling in Deeper
"Dirty Wicked" (novella)
A Very Wicked Christmas (short story)
Holding on Tighter

THE DEVOTED LOVERS
Devoted to Pleasure
Devoted to Wicked (novella)
Devoted to Love

THE PERFECT GENTLEMEN (by Shayla Black and Lexi Blake) (Complete Series)
Scandal Never Sleeps
Seduction in Session
Big Easy Temptation
Smoke and Sin
At the Pleasure of the President

MASTERS OF Ménage (by Shayla Black and Lexi Blake)
Their Virgin Captive
Their Virgin's Secret
Their Virgin Concubine
Their Virgin Princess
Their Virgin Hostage
Their Virgin Secretary
Their Virgin Mistress

DOMS OF HER LIFE (by Shayla Black, Jenna Jacob, and Isabella LaPearl)
Raine Falling Collection (Complete Saga)
One Dom To Love
The Young And The Submissive
The Bold and The Dominant
The Edge of Dominance

Heavenly Rising Collection
The Choice
The Chase
Coming Soon:
The Commitment (2021)

More Than Protect You

A More Than Words Novella

By Shayla Black

1001 DARK NIGHTS
PRESS

More Than Protect You: A More Than Words Novella
Copyright 2020 Shelley Bradley LLC
ISBN: 978-1-970077-92-6

Foreword: Copyright 2014 M. J. Rose

Cover photo credit © Annie Ray/ Passion Pages

Published by 1001 Dark Nights Press, an imprint of Evil Eye
Concepts, Incorporated

Foreword from the Author

There are infinite ways to tell someone you love them. Some of the most powerful don't require words at all. This was the truth rolling through my head when I first conceived of this series, writing about a love so complete that mere letters strung together to make sentences weren't an adequate communicator of those feelings. Music is one of my go-to choices.

I *love* music. I'm always immersed in it and spend hours a day with my earbuds plugged in. I write to music. I think to music. I even sleep to music. I was thrilled to incorporate songs into the story I felt were meaningful to the journey. I think of it this way: a movie has a soundtrack. Why shouldn't a book?

So I created one.

Some of the songs I've selected will be familiar. Some are old. Some are newer. Some popular. Some obscure. They all just fit (in my opinion) and came straight from the heart. I listened to many of these songs as I wrote the book.

For maximum understanding (and feels), I recommend becoming familiar with these songs and either playing them or rolling them around in your head as you read. Due to copyright laws, I can't use exact lyrics, but I tried to give you the gist of those most meaningful to the story. I've also made it simple for you to give them a listen by creating a Spotify playlist.

YOU GIVE LOVE A BAD NAME - Bon Jovi
HEART-SHAPED BOX - Nirvana
WOMAN, AMEN - Dierks Bentley
DON'T SPEAK - No Doubt
SPEECHLESS - Dan + Shay

Sign up for the 1001 Dark Nights Newsletter
and be entered to win a Tiffany Key necklace.

There's a contest every month!

Go to www.1001DarkNights.com to subscribe.

**As a bonus, all subscribers can download
FIVE FREE exclusive books!**

One Thousand and One Dark Nights

Once upon a time, in the future…

*I was a student fascinated with stories and learning.
I studied philosophy, poetry, history, the occult, and
the art and science of love and magic. I had a vast
library at my father's home and collected thousands
of volumes of fantastic tales.*

*I learned all about ancient races and bygone
times. About myths and legends and dreams of all
people through the millennium. And the more I read
the stronger my imagination grew until I discovered
that I was able to travel into the stories... to actually
become part of them.*

*I wish I could say that I listened to my teacher
and respected my gift, as I ought to have. If I had, I
would not be telling you this tale now.
But I was foolhardy and confused, showing off
with bravery.*

*One afternoon, curious about the myth of the
Arabian Nights, I traveled back to ancient Persia to
see for myself if it was true that every day Shahryar
(Persian: شهريار, "king") married a new virgin, and then
sent yesterday's wife to be beheaded. It was written
and I had read that by the time he met Scheherazade,
the vizier's daughter, he'd killed one thousand
women.*

Something went wrong with my efforts. I arrived in the midst of the story and somehow exchanged places with Scheherazade — a phenomena that had never occurred before and that still to this day, I cannot explain.

Now I am trapped in that ancient past. I have taken on Scheherazade's life and the only way I can protect myself and stay alive is to do what she did to protect herself and stay alive.

Every night the King calls for me and listens as I spin tales. And when the evening ends and dawn breaks, I stop at a point that leaves him breathless and yearning for more. And so the King spares my life for one more day, so that he might hear the rest of my dark tale.

As soon as I finish a story... I begin a new one... like the one that you, dear reader, have before you now.

Chapter One

Tanner

There's nothing like Bon Jovi waking me up before five a.m. on a Sunday morning. I eye my phone, now blasting "You Give Love a Bad Name," my soon-to-be ex-wife's ringtone. She only ever calls when she wants something, so this ought to be interesting.

I grope the device off the nightstand and flop back to my pillow. "What, Ellie?"

"It's *Elise* now."

The day I met her, working on a ranch a hundred miles outside of Pueblo, Colorado, she was Ellie. She was a happy-go-lucky nineteen and didn't have an uncompromising thought in her head. I took one look at her sloppy ponytail, hazel eyes, crooked smile, and very short shorts—and I fell. We got married a few years later, bought a house, and started a business together. Everything was going all right...until it wasn't. Eight years had gone by when I looked up and realized I was married to a stranger. When she asked for a trial separation, I didn't fight. That night, I packed a bag and walked out the door. I haven't missed her since.

"Do you know what fucking time it is in Maui, *Elise*?"

"Early. I know. But since you haven't been available during reasonable daytime hours lately, I thought I'd try this."

So me ignoring her three phone calls yesterday wasn't subtle enough? "What do you want?"

"Did you get the paperwork yet? I signed it. The carrier shows it was delivered to you on Friday."

She's itching for our divorce to be final. In truth, I'm feeling the same. We separated nearly two years ago, and finally this long road is almost over.

"Yeah."

"And? Is that all you have to say?"

"Yeah." Mostly because it drives her crazy. I'm not trying to antagonize her simply to be a vengeful asshole. I'm just hoping if these phone calls are painful enough she'll stop.

She sighs like she's grappling for patience. "Tanner Maxwell Kirk, please give me a straightforward answer once and for all. Are you going to sign the papers?"

"Yeah." Why would I stay married to her now?

"This week?"

"You in a hurry?" I ask out of curiosity more than anything. And maybe because I want to yank her chain.

"Not that you care, but yes."

"Why? You're not looking to get married again, are you?"

She hesitates. "I don't see that it's any of your business."

"Then I don't see why I have to sign right away."

"Ugh, you are the most frustrating, infuriating man! I only married you because I wanted off that damn ranch, and I didn't know how damaging the traditional, patriarchal institution of marriage was…"

I tune out. I've heard this speech. She didn't find marriage demeaning or oppressive until she decided to go back to college and took a bunch of classes that turned her thinking inside out. Fine. I never wanted to hold her back. The moment she asked, I set her free. A few months later, I even hired an attorney to make it official.

I interrupt her diatribe. "Just answer my question and I'll sign."

Ellie sighs. "Not exactly."

"Then what?"

"Is it any of your business?" she huffs. "I don't ask who you've fucked lately."

"Actually, you did. About a month ago."

"I'd had too much to drink that night. I just wanted to make sure you're getting on with your life."

Riiight… "Seems like you got interested in my sex life not long after I moved out and got one that didn't include you."

She finally drops the attitude. "Caring is a hard habit to break. We were together for so long…"

"And then you decided we weren't because I was oppressing you or whatever."

"Not *you* specifically, though you have your overbearing moments."

She's mentioned that about a hundred times. "You want me to apologize for caring about you?"

"It felt more like hovering. But in this case, I meant the institution of marriage. I just couldn't be the feminist I know I am now and yet remain in a practice I don't believe in anymore. It didn't mean I stopped having feelings."

But it did mean we stopped having sex. And I'm over this conversation. "I wish you nothing but the best, Ellie, whatever your plans may be. I'll sign the papers and drop them back in the mail to my attorney tomorrow. As soon as the judge processes them and the house sells, you'll be free of me."

"Thank you. I'm entering into a domestic partnership."

"What's his name?"

"Patricia."

Okay, *that* shocks me. "You're in a relationship with another woman?"

"It just...happened. I'd been seeing a fellow grad student. Scott was nice. He liked antiquing, classical music, and photography."

Everything I don't. Yet she still wasn't happy?

"He introduced me to his sister over lunch one day, and I realized people don't truly fall in love with the body; they fall in love with the soul. Patricia has the most beautiful soul. But I'm scared, Tanner. She's a lot smarter. She knows herself so much better. She seems sure of everything."

And Ellie is still trying to find herself. I finally figured that out. She looked for her identity as my wife. When that failed, she tried to pin it on motherhood. When her ovaries wouldn't cooperate, she tried to find meaning in being a student. Now she's looking for some pinnacle of self-actualization in a same-sex partnership. I don't know Patricia, but I already feel sorry for her. In a few years, Ellie will drift away, and Patricia will probably only have the faintest idea why.

"You didn't ask for my advice, and at the risk of being overbearing, I'm going to suggest you give her your all. Communicate. Invest your heart this time. Focus not on what you can't have but what you can."

She's quiet for such a long time, I'm worried she's pissed. "You're probably right. I never meant to hurt you."

"I know."

"And I'm sorry."

"I know." Just like I know this will be one of the last conversations we ever have. It's sad…but that's life. We've both moved on.

"You going to stay in Maui?"

"Probably. I'm looking into opening a shooting range here. I've found a good location. All I have to do is sign the lease." And come up with the money to start a new business. Right now, that's a tall order. I'm flat broke.

"Where are you going to live?"

"Once the house sells, I can buy a condo on the island or something."

"You staying with Joe?" she asks about my buddy Camden's dad.

"At his place. He's away on business now." But he's due back tomorrow night, so I need to find somewhere else to crash ASAP that won't cost me a fortune. His studio apartment isn't big enough for both of us. "The good news is, I've met a few of his fishing buddies and found some good restaurants. I'm enjoying the island. It's a start."

"Good luck. I hope you find the right someone to spend your life with. I hope she can give you children because I know you want them. And I hope you're deliriously happy. As far as husbands go, you were mostly decent."

From Ellie, that's high praise, but I'm done with marriage, wanting kids, and the illusion of happily ever after. "Thanks. Good luck, El."

Three beeps tell me she's gone, probably for good.

It seems odd that what started during a chilly fall night is now ending on a warm spring dawn. Maybe that timing ought to tell me something…

With a sigh, I rise. Since I'm up now, I'll go ahead and grab a shower.

Three minutes later, I'm toweling off and padding back to my duffel for some clothes. It's too early on a Sunday to be looking for work, so I might as well go fishing. Once I've tossed on some shorts and a tank, I drag Joe's fishing gear from the corner and search for my shoes.

My phone rings again, the run-of-the-mill ringtone. I almost brush it off, but a glance at the display tells me it's someone I actually want to talk to. "Hey, Trace. Good to hear from you. Looking for a fishing buddy this morning?"

"I wish. I have a prospective client who wants to meet you, like, now."

The gravity in his voice tells me he's got a situation and it's serious. I shove the fishing gear back in the corner. "What's up?"

"I'm calling on behalf of a family friend. Amanda is twenty-six. Single mother to a boy about to turn one. The father of her baby is…notorious."

Interesting choice of words. "Sounds like you're putting it nicely. Is she worried he's coming back for her?"

"No, thank God. He's not violent; he's dead. But his enemies are after her."

So they can't accept that the cause of their anger is gone and chose instead to take it out on a woman? This is why people annoy me.

"I'm happy to do what I can. But I have to be honest. I haven't done any bodyguarding in a while."

"And I know you're just getting settled on the island. I wouldn't ask…but I don't know anyone else with your skill set. I'm sure they're out there, but they'd be a stranger I don't know if I can trust. These scumbags are threatening her kid's life, too. Could you protect them?"

I can't do it for long since I need to find a steady job. I'm also not sure where I can take them that's safe. But I'll figure it out. I can't let this woman and her kid live in fear. And will they live at all if I don't intervene? "For a few days. While I'm finding her someone more competent. I'll teach her a bit of self-defense, too."

Once I'm gone, it might keep her safe.

"Perfect. Thanks, man. I owe you."

"No problem. Where is she now?"

"I'm going to give you her half-sister's address. She's been staying there, but obviously she can't anymore. Nia is thirty weeks pregnant and—"

"Say no more. If you can help me figure out a place to hide Amanda, I'll take it from there."

"I'll ask around and see if I can have something worked out shortly. Just get over here as soon as you can. I don't feel right leaving Amanda and her son alone here with Nia, but my son is with a…friend, so I need to get home."

My guess? The friend is more than a friend. Who but a lover would be at his place at five a.m.? But Trace having female company hardly surprises me. His older brother, Noah Weston, the former pro quarterback, is well known for scoring on the field. Trace has a reputation for scoring off of it.

He's put some effort into his sex life. You might try that, dude, before your penis forgets why it exists.

Telling the voice in my head to shut the hell up, I grab my shades, my Glock, and the keys to Joe's classic red Mustang. He told me if I could fix it, I could drive it while he was gone. A few hours and a few parts later, I had her purring like a kitten.

GPS and Nirvana guide me to an address on the western side of the island. It's a multi-million dollar house situated right on the ocean. As I pull up, the place is ablaze with lights. I let loose a low whistle. Amanda's half-sister, whoever she is, lives in paradise.

Out front, I see Trace talking to an attractive brunette. As I step from the car, he waves. "Hey, Tanner."

"How you doing?" I lock the Mustang, then greet him with a handshake and a shoulder bump.

"Okay. Thanks for coming so early and on such short notice."

"No problem. I'm not okay with a mob harassing women and children." I glance at the brunette. "You Amanda?"

"No, I'm Harlow."

"She's my brother's wife," Trace supplies.

I haven't met Trace's famous brother, but his wife's friendly smile tells me she's super down-to-earth. "Nice to meet you." I shake her hand, then turn back to Trace. "Where's Amanda?"

I need to find her, start asking questions, and figure out my best course of action. As I drove up, a glance told me people trampled the flowers around the perimeter of the house and broke a window out front. I need to get Amanda out of here and stash her someplace both secret and safe.

A beautiful African American woman approaches down the front walkway, dressed in a white silk robe and looking very pregnant. "She's inside. Her son is cranky since his sleep has been disrupted. She's trying to get him back down. I'm Nia Cook."

I shake her hand and introduce myself. "Nice to meet you. Can I go in and talk to her? I'd like to start getting a feel for how I can best help."

"Sure. She's at the back of the house, down the hall, first door on the left."

"Thanks." I glance over at Trace. "Catch up with you later?"

"Yeah. I'll figure out a location and call you. Good to see you, man."

"You, too. We'll have to go fishing again soon."

With the niceties exchanged, I head into the big house, cursing under my breath at the broken glass in the living room. As I head down the hall, I hear a fussing child's voice.

"*No!*"

"Oliver, calm down, buddy. Everything is fine. Just fine…" a woman soothes.

Quietly, I tread closer, pausing just outside the bedroom. I don't want to startle her since she and the boy have had an eventful night, but there's something about her voice… It lures me in. It's melodic as it caresses my senses. But it's also steely enough to warn me against mistaking her softness for weakness.

I haven't even seen this woman, but anticipation flares across my skin. It burns through my veins.

"That's a good boy," she murmurs as I turn the corner to look at her.

I freeze in my tracks.

A waifish blonde, seemingly swallowed up by soft cotton pajamas two sizes too big in a blue so pale they almost look white, stands over a playpen. Her profile is hidden by her long waves as she bends, pacifier in one dainty, outstretched hand.

Without even glimpsing her face, I'm riveted. I don't register anything or anyone else for breathless, interminable moments.

Finally, I blink. I have to stop staring. If I can't, there's no fucking way I'll be able to keep her safe.

"Amanda?"

With a soft gasp, she whirls to me, seeming to search for words. "A-are you Tanner Kirk?"

I stare at her bare face and her pouty, parted lips. She's beautiful and wary. And she looks so fucking young.

"Yeah." I stick out my hand. "Hi."

She folds her much-smaller palm against mine. At the contact, she stiffens. I do my best to ignore the lash of heat that singes my palm and snakes up my arm. Any chance she's feeling this crazy reaction, too?

"Thank you for coming. Nice to meet you."

I nod. "Likewise."

To stop myself from gawking at her soft face and even softer blue eyes, I turn my attention to the boy. He has a sharp jaw that's nothing like Amanda's…and a headful of pale curls that are. He stands in the middle of a playpen with red cheeks, glowering green eyes, and little fists.

"That's Oliver, my son."

"You're not happy, big guy?"

The boy rears back at me with an angry furrow between his brows. "No."

Beside me, Amanda sighs. "It's one of the two words he knows right now."

"What's the other?"

"Ma ma." He holds out his arms to her.

"No." She shakes her head softly. "Sleep."

The boy gets angrier, stomping his foot and huffing.

"I don't think he's going to take no for an answer," I remark.

"He'll wear himself out eventually. I hate to leave him because I don't want him to be afraid."

"Do you think he understands what happened here earlier?"

"No, thank goodness."

But she's terrified. Oh, she's trying to be brave. I can tell by the way she squares her shoulders and lifts her chin. If she wants comfort, it doesn't show. I admire that, even as I want to put my arms around her and tell her I'll take care of everything. I don't for two reasons. First, Ellie resented my "macho BS." And second, I just met Amanda. But after my reaction to her, if I'm going to protect her I have no business touching her.

"We can stay and talk here, if that makes you more comfortable. I'd just like to ask you some questions."

She shakes her head. "If we stay, he'll never sleep. Do you mind if we talk in the next room? I'll be close enough to hear him, but…"

Far enough away that her son won't be distracted. "No problem. Lead the way."

"Come here, little man." She bends to him again. When he lifts his arms to her, she folds him against her chest and holds him tight for a precious moment, kissing the top of his head before stepping away. "Now go to sleep. Or no trucks when you wake up."

He stomps his foot again, but to her credit she ignores his tantrum and heads for the door, turning off the recessed lights overhead and ensuring his nightlight snaps on to illuminate the shadows.

"Ma ma!" Oliver sounds mad.

"Sleep tight," she croons. "Mama loves you."

When I file out, she breezes into the hall and guides me to the bedroom next door. Her bed looks barely slept in, and I wonder how exhausted she must be. Her suitcase sits in the corner on a luggage rack. Other than that, it appears as if she's hardly stepped foot in here.

"Thank you for coming so quickly." She sits on the edge of the bed, then gestures me to a plush chair nearby. "And thank you for your patience."

She's unfailingly polite. Have tonight's events rattled her...or do I make her nervous? Either way, I need to set her at ease now or we're going to have a long few days together. But that won't be easy. Every time I look at Amanda, I think things I shouldn't. There's something about her I've never encountered. She's so soft and female—seemingly vulnerable—but I'm seeing that when it counts, she's strong.

And the way she's looking at me, like I'm the answer to her problems, only makes the tug of attraction between us stronger. Or maybe that's in my head?

"I'm just sorry things got so out of hand that you need me here," I say as I sit.

"I didn't expect that. I'd had this problem in California, where my son's father ruined more lives than mine. But now that he's gone...I seem to be the next best target. I never imagined these people would follow me across an ocean."

Since I have no idea who her son's father was or what's going on, I have to ask. "I hate to make you tread old ground, but do you mind clueing me in? When Trace called me, he was short on details. To protect you, I need to understand the threat."

She gives me another of those oh-so-polite smiles. "I figured this was coming. Do you know who Barclay Reed was?"

"Sorry. No."

"Head of Reed Financial. He was an investment broker to a lot of wealthy people. I was his assistant for a couple of years, starting right out of college, though I'd known him most of my life. Our fathers were, I thought, the best of friends."

"Your father?"

"Douglas Lund, head of Colossus Investment Corporation."

I've never heard of him either, but clearly she grew up wealthy. "Go on. And Barclay Reed fathered your son?"

"Yes."

If he was her father's best friend, how much older was this guy? "I see."

"Just like I see you doing the mental math. Everyone does. I was twenty-four when I got pregnant. Barclay was fifty-seven. How it happened is a long story. I won't bore you."

A long story…how? "Did he rape you?"

She presses her lips together. "You're not the first person to ask. No. Unfortunately, I was naive and very willing."

I can't imagine how or why this beauty would have allowed a man more than twice her age into her bed, but it's none of my business. I'm here because she and her son are in danger, so I shelve my curiosity—and my more than vague sense of annoyance that this guy touched her.

"What do the attacks have to do with Barclay Reed?"

"In a nutshell, he swindled all of his clients out of their fortunes and was arrested for it last June. He left them all virtually penniless. I had no idea what Barclay had done. When the FBI raided his offices, I was recovering from childbirth. But Barclay had let me go months before that. Shortly after I told him I was pregnant, in fact. Still, I'd been his most recent mistress, so when he was arrested, the media had a field day with our 'salacious' affair."

"He was married at the time?"

"Yes. He had been for nearly thirty-five years."

She doesn't bat an eye. Doesn't blink. In fact, nothing Amanda says tells me how she feels, but disillusionment and heartache simmer under her surface. She cared about Barclay Reed. Despite the fact he stole from others, cheated on his wife, and used her, she had feelings for the scumbag.

Why?

I don't understand, but it's not my place to judge. I need to stop letting this sudden, stupid interest blindside me and do what I promised.

Amanda sends me a tight smile. "I see what you're thinking. It's what everyone thinks. How could you sleep with a married man your father's age? I had my reasons. They're my own. I also have sins I'll have to live with for the rest of my life. And if I had a do-over, no. I wouldn't change a thing because Barclay gave me Oliver. He's my world now. But I would like the peace of mind of knowing I can keep my son safe."

"Of course. I'll make sure nothing happens to either of you. What does this mob want?"

She shrugs. "Revenge, I guess. Barclay's oldest daughter, Bethany, worked as his right hand. She didn't know anything, either. She's already returned all the money to his former clients since she recovered it, so these people aren't after cash. And I don't have any information to give them. They assume that Barclay's secrets were our pillow talk, but he told me almost nothing. And the few things he did say were lies. I shared what I thought I knew with the FBI. When they were done laughing, they dismissed me."

Every word carries a brittle edge. She made some bad decisions. The man she trusted betrayed her. Then life chewed her up and spit her out. I've had a shitty few years, too, but hers have been far worse. I've also got a dozen years more experience handling bullshit. She was barely a young adult when her world blew up in her face.

"I'm sorry."

She softens and shakes her head. "I apologize if I seem bitter."

"How do you think the angry hoard found you?"

She sighs. "I should have guessed this was the first place people would look. Nia is my half-sister; we share a father. Long story. But that's not the only connection. Evan, her husband, and Oliver are both Barclay's illegitimate sons."

Not only was the thief a habitual cheat, but her own father couldn't keep it in his pants, either? Nice. "Since you have connections to both Mr. and Mrs. Cook…"

"People assumed I would come here after leaving California."

I make a mental note that any safe house for Amanda can't be with family—on either side. "We'll get you to safety soon."

"Thank you. But I can't hide forever. I won't. I hear you're a firearms instructor."

"Yeah. I owned a range in Colorado for about ten years. I've taught for longer than that."

"You don't own the range anymore?"

I shake my head. "Sold it when I filed for divorce awhile back."

"I'm sorry."

"Don't be. My soon-to-be-ex and I are both much happier. And I'm thinking about opening a range in Maui soon."

"When did you move here?"

"I really haven't yet, but I think I'm going to."

A little furrow appears between her brows. "Maybe I should consider a move, too. I can't go back to LA. And I won't go to New York, where I grew up. My father still lives there. I don't need his meddling. Hell"—she tosses her hands in the air—"maybe I'll stay here, too. My brother, Stephen, just relocated to the island for his wife,

Skye."

"You two close?"

"Yeah. He's always been there for me, especially when my dad wasn't."

"Did your dad travel a lot or something when you were a kid?"

I should stop asking irrelevant personal questions. It's none of my business, and has no bearing on how I protect Amanda. But they keep slipping out of my mouth. I can't deny I'm curious.

"I suppose, but that wasn't really the problem. He can be a real bastard, which is probably why he and Barclay were friends. Stephen assures me Dad has mellowed with age. Maybe." She shrugs. "Anyway, while we're together, I was hoping you could teach me to shoot. I'll pay you."

"Sure."

"If it wasn't clear, I'll pay you for all your time."

"I appreciate that, but I can only stay a few days."

Amanda shakes her head, and it's impossible not to notice the way her pale waves skim over breasts that I'd bet a hundred bucks aren't restrained by a bra.

"Then you should go. I need someone who's willing to commit a bit longer."

Maybe so, but... "Who else are you going to find at barely six a.m. on a Sunday morning?"

"I don't know, but I need someone for more than a day or two."

"And I need a steady, long-term job. You're going to want someone with more experience, anyway. But I'll be here until we can find you that guy."

"Fine." She doesn't sound happy about it. "How much would it take to entice you to stay for the week?"

"We'll work it out." Normally, I wouldn't let a negotiation go. It's stupid and irresponsible to agree to work before coming to financial terms, but Amanda, despite holding her own and standing up for herself, looks exhausted. And I feel like shit for wondering what she looks like under those pajamas. Even now, I'm picturing her. I have no doubt her body would both take my breath away and kick my libido into overdrive.

Stop being a lech, dude. Do your job.

"Why don't you go back to sleep while Oliver seems to be out?" I suggest. "That will give me time to figure out where I can take you that's safe."

She shakes her head. "I'll need to pack and find a crib or playpen for my son. I can't take Nia's. She'll need it soon."

Probably not in the next few days, but I sense Amanda hates imposing on anyone, even her own family.

"All right, if you change your mind…"

"I won't. Coffee?"

"Sure. Black, please. I'm going to walk the perimeter and find Trace."

She nods my way, then shoulders past me and pads down the hall. I try not to notice that the top of her head only reaches my shoulder or that she's got a lush, round ass, visible even under the too-big pajama pants. I definitely try to ignore my ill-timed erection.

Note to self: Find someone else to bodyguard her ASAP. She's a distraction I don't need.

Easier said than done. Who the fuck else do I know on Maui? I've only been here eight days.

Cursing under my breath, I head out the back of the house, glimpse more evidence of the angry crowd, then head for Trace. He's still talking to Harlow and Nia when I stroll up.

"How did it go with Amanda?"

"Fine." What else am I supposed to say? *Why didn't you tell me she's so gorgeous it would fuck with my head?*

"Good." Trace nods. "I've been giving the safe house situation some thought. I have an idea, but I need to talk to someone. Give me a couple of hours?"

"Sure." I figure no one will come back in broad daylight. Bitching mobs are usually made up of cowards who prefer to slink under the cover of dark. "We just need to get out of here before sundown."

Trace grimaces. "You think that's soon enough? The guy who broke into the house last night—"

"What?" That's the first I'm hearing of an intruder.

"Yeah."

Nia adds her two cents. "He cornered Amanda in the hall and threatened her. He had a knife. If she hadn't—"

"Knife? Fuck! We need to leave—now."

"And go where?" Trace asks.

No idea. "I'll think of something." I turn to Nia. "I need a connection for a crib or playpen. She won't take yours."

"I figured. I'll make some phone calls. I think Griff and Britta have a spare."

No idea who they are, and right now, I don't care. "Thanks. One of you let me know when you have some information."

"Sure." Trace nods.

I'm barely listening as I haul ass back inside. Amanda shouldn't be alone right now. Neither should Oliver, not until the threat is behind bars.

I find Amanda in the kitchen, watching the drip of the coffeemaker. "You didn't tell me there was an intruder."

She raises her brows at my accusing tone. "You didn't ask. Besides, I handled him with a swift kick to the balls and a vase over the head."

This little thing took on someone unhinged enough to break in with a knife and the intent to kill? "You *what?*"

"Yes. What was I supposed to do?" She cocks a hand on her hip. "I wasn't letting him anywhere near my son."

I'm both horrified and impressed. "Call 911 before they're in your face."

Amanda shakes her head. "Even if I had, the police would have come too late."

I see her point...I just don't like it. "You don't have to worry about that anymore. I'm here. Get your stuff. We're going."

"But Oliver—"

"Can sleep later. Get it. I'll stand over you until you're done. Now move."

Chapter Two

In fifteen minutes, Amanda manages to pack everything up in two rolling suitcases and a diaper bag. She hugs Nia and Harlow, both of whom glare suspiciously. Now that I'm hustling Amanda out the door, they're obviously skeptical that calling me was a good idea. I'm not trying to be an asshole, but they don't understand. A nut job willing to break in and kill with a knife is far more serious than a chanting, flower-trampling mob.

"Is this everything?" I ask, taking hold of Amanda's luggage.

She hoists her son against her chest. He's obviously going to be a big boy. Against her small frame, he looks massive. "Yes."

"Then let's go."

When I turn, Nia grabs my sleeve. "Where are you taking her?"

"Someplace temporary."

"You need to be more forthcoming. I can't let you just take her wherever when there's someone out to kill her."

"With all due respect, if this would-be killer comes for her again, he'll come here first. If he thinks you know where she is, he'll threaten you. Since Amanda thwarted him the first time, he'll come more prepared. Trace says your husband is in London."

"Yes."

Nia clearly doesn't like what I'm saying. Too bad. That won't change my message.

"Then I suggest you find somewhere else to stay until he comes home. You're not safe, either." Then I reach for Amanda, put a guiding hand to the small of her back, and nudge her toward the Mustang.

"Be careful. I'll call you," she promises Nia over her shoulder.

"Please. I'll be worried. We're supposed to have lunch with Skye and Stephen today. What do you want me to tell them?"

"Damn it. Um, tell them Oliver has the sniffles." She turns to me. "Is the car seat set up?"

Trace said he'd do it before he left. I assume he knows how. I sure as hell don't. "Should be."

A minute later, Amanda straps in her sleepy son, then slips into the front seat. As I get behind the wheel, she sticks her head out the window at Nia, now standing on the porch, watching us. "I forgot my purse. Will you grab it for me? It's in the kitchen."

"Getting it." She darts back in the house, white robe swishing behind her.

She emerges a minute later, absently caressing her belly and carrying a small shoulder bag. She approaches Amanda and hands her the purse.

Then she bends to glare at me. "If anything happens to her, I'll be pissed as hell. But if you hurt one hair on her head, they'll need tweezers to find all the parts of your body." Then she turns to her half-sister. They might look like polar opposites, but they clearly have strong backbones in common. "Take care, honey. Call me if you need anything."

"I will." Amanda squeezes her hand. "Please don't worry about me. I don't want you stressed and upsetting your little one."

"Bye."

Finally, I drive off. As we leave Nia's neighborhood, the sun begins climbing the sky. If anyone is watching the house, they'll see me taking Amanda away. In a car like this, we won't be hard to follow.

I'm going to need to stash this vehicle quickly.

"Now what?" she asks over my music as she rolls up her window.

"For now, we go to the apartment where I've been staying. I need to pack up. While we're there, I'll see if I can find a safe house. Trace is looking, too. As soon as something pops, we'll get over there and hunker down."

"Fine. Can you turn that—I guess you'd call it music—down?" She glances back at Oliver. The poor kid is so worn out he's sleeping through every note.

I adjust the volume. "You don't like 'Heart-Shaped Box'? Or are you objecting to Kurt Cobain?"

"I've never heard this song, and I don't know who you're talking about."

Is she kidding right now? "Kurt Cobain, lead singer of Nirvana?"
She shrugs. "Sorry."

"No. I didn't realize..." But it makes sense once I think about it.
Was she even alive when he died?

There's roughly a dozen years that form the chasm between our
ages. This is a shitty reminder. With a shake of my head, I sigh.

"How do you listen to that stuff?" she asks. "It's depressing."

"I grew up with it. Since today is the anniversary of Cobain's
death, it felt apropos to play some Nirvana, but...who are you into?
Charlie Puth? Or are you more of a Taylor Swift type?"

She looks at me like I'm somewhere between crazy and insulting.
"I'm not sixteen anymore."

"So what do you like?"

"Luke Combs. Dierks Bentley." She sighs and pats her heart.
"Jake Owen and Blake Shelton."

Aren't those guys more my age? "You like...country music?"

"A lot of people do." She's defensive, and I never meant to make
her feel that way.

"Sure." Even though I grew up in Colorado, and folks I knew
who worked on ranches played it, I never listened to it much myself.

"But I grew up with classical music," she goes on. "My mother
had anxiety issues, and that helped to calm her."

"If you grew up in New York, where did you first hear country?"

"In grade school, I had a friend originally from Texas. Katie loved
it, so I started listening to it with her. She moved away again a few
years later, but my parents hated the 'twangy' stuff. So I kept listening.
And"—she shrugs—"I just never stopped."

Under her buttoned-up façade, she's a bit of a rebel. That doesn't
surprise me, but I would have never guessed that little Miss Privileged
was into songs about pickup trucks, breakups, and beer. "Is there even
a country station on the island?"

"I haven't been here long enough to find out."

"When did you leave LA?" I ask, navigating the thin Sunday
morning traffic back to the north side.

"Four days ago."

She doesn't say more, and the subject is closed. It's for the best.
We need to get down to business.

"Had you received death threats back in Cali?"

"Of course. More than one."

Fuck. "Had anyone broken into your place?"

"They couldn't. I lived in a high-security building. You can't even operate the elevator without a card key. But I couldn't stay in my apartment forever. And once Oliver started running a few weeks ago, he went stir crazy if I didn't take him to the park at least once a day. But the minute I stepped out of my building, it was a zoo, especially right after Barclay was killed."

So she'd exchanged security for distance, hoping she could have a life, and it hadn't worked out? "Who killed him?"

"A former client named Paul Daniels." She shakes her head. "I know what you're thinking, and he isn't the one threatening me now. Not only was he in jail, he died of cancer last month."

"Do you have any idea who else might want to kill you? Do you know the name of anyone who's threatened you?"

"No. Most threats came online."

"Keyboard warriors are always brave when they're hiding behind screen names."

"A few more antagonistic people came to yell in my face. But the police never took any of them seriously. Most of the time they had no plan, no weapon… They decided 'I'll kill you' was a figure of speech."

That's not a surprise, but since someone had tried to gut her last night? "I'm not. I'm taking this very seriously."

"Thanks. I'm just sorry I don't know anything."

"If you remember anyone who threatened you more than once or followed you somewhere—anything sinister or scary—let me know." I have a feeling *someone* fits that description, but with everything she's been through in the last few hours, she can't remember.

"Maybe it's a former client of Barclay's who lives on Maui and decided to take advantage of the situation while I'm here?"

"Did he have clients in Maui?"

"I don't know." She glances away, almost as if she doesn't want to look me in the face. "We didn't talk business much."

I get the feeling they didn't talk a lot in general, and she's embarrassed by that. "How would anyone have known you were here in Maui? Did you put it on social media?"

She shakes her head. "I deactivated all my accounts when my relationship with Barclay became public after his arrest, and I didn't tell anyone I was coming except my dad and my brother."

And who knows if they told anyone else. I sigh as I pull up to Joe's apartment building. It's two stories, painted a garish turquoise blue, and sitting up on a hill surrounded by a retaining wall made of rock. The inside is even less special…except the nice view of the Pacific three blocks away.

"Who does this place belong to?"

"A friend's dad. Let's go."

"I don't want to wake Oliver." She looks back at him. "He's just fallen asleep."

"I can't leave you two outside while I pack, and I need you someplace safe where I can think. Pick him up and—" When she grimaces, I sigh. "What's the problem?"

"He's getting too big for me to wrangle out of his car seat without waking him."

"You want me to do it?"

"Would you?"

If it will get her out of the parking lot, where any asshole with a gun could shoot her, and into a safer space, I don't have much choice.

"I'll try. No promises." Especially since I know nothing about kids.

She eases out of the car, purse slung over her shoulder. "I appreciate the help."

I nod—and try not to stare. Since I gave her three minutes to change before we left Nia's place, Amanda isn't wearing anything particularly interesting—a white T-shirt tied in a knot at her navel, a pair of faded cutoffs, a pink ball cap, and a matching pair of flip-flops. But it shows off the curve of her breasts, her small waist, and the long expanse of her tanned thighs. It shouldn't be sexy…but she gives me another instant erection.

Jesus, as soon as I'm done guarding her body, I need to get laid.

Muttering a curse, I flip up the front seat of the two-door coupe, then unbuckle the sleeping boy from his seat. He barely stirs as I lift him against my chest. I have to admit, he weighs more than I expected. No wonder a little thing like her is having trouble.

"Follow me."

She nods, then I head across the parking lot and down the east side of the building to Joe's front door. Oliver smells like sunshine, grass, and Cheerios. It's not altogether unpleasant. Then he flings an arm over my shoulder and turns his head until his nose is half-buried in my neck.

Okay, I admit it. He's actually cute. But that's another distraction I don't need.

When we reach Joe's door, I juggle the boy long enough to shove the key in the lock, then I wave Amanda inside, scan my surroundings once more, and shut the door. As I flip the deadbolt, her phone starts buzzing in her purse.

Easing Oliver onto the rumpled bed, I turn as she pulls the device free. "Who is it?"

Any chance her would-be killer is someone she knows? Someone now trying to track her down?

"My brother. I'm sure he's worried."

If he has any intention of coming around and mucking up my arrangements, it's a no from me.

I gesture to her. "You can answer it, but you can't tell him where you are. The fewer people who know, the better."

She presses her lips together before she takes the call. "Hi, Stephen. Are you home from the hospital? How are Skye and the baby? Is she still spotting?" After a brief pause, she interrupts. "No. Stop. I'm fine. Oliver is fine." Another pause. "That didn't happen." And another. "I wasn't going to call you in the middle of the night when I knew you and Skye were at the ER. Nia and I are big girls. We handled it."

I don't know what he's saying to her, but I can hear his deep voice and seeming agitation across the room.

"No. I'm not coming to stay with you. I refuse to put either of you at risk. Skye doesn't need more problems right now, especially ones she didn't create. She needs you to focus on her and the baby. I've got a bodyguard named Tanner. I'm with him. I'll be fine." Her brother spits something less than calm through the phone, and she rolls her eyes. "Why? I don't see what good that will do."

Amanda listens, now pacing from one side of the small studio apartment to the other, seemingly gearing up to defend herself again. What the hell? Doesn't he think Amanda has been through enough?

Her family shit is none of your business.

After all, they have wealth. I'll bet they have the connections to go with it. I know how ruthlessly people like that operate. I can't afford to get tangled up in their strife.

"Fine." She pries the phone from her ear and presses the mute button. "He wants to talk to you."

That, I didn't expect.

Reluctantly, I hold out my hand, hoping he just has basic questions. "All right. Sit down. Relax. Water?"

The only other thing in Joe's fridge is beer.

"No thanks." She hands me the phone. "Just…he means well."

If that's true, why is she wringing her hands?

I unmute the phone. "Tanner Kirk here."

"Who the fuck are you? Hours after she's attacked, I finally find out. Someone should have called me. I'm her brother. I live on the island, but I'm finding out last? What the hell is going on?"

Yep, he's pissed, but he's obviously concerned, too. "I got a phone call a couple of hours ago from a mutual friend that your sister was the target of a gang bent on violence, and I agreed to help." I don't mention the intruder since I'm pretty sure nothing would keep him from coming if he knew. "I've done some bodyguarding in the past, and I'm a firearms instructor. I've agreed to teach Amanda how to shoot. I'll be keeping her in a secure location. You can call her anytime you like, but I won't disclose to anyone where we're going."

"I'm not sure who our supposed 'mutual friend' is, but I don't know a damn thing about you, so no. You're not keeping my sister's location a secret from me. And you better not touch her, pal. She's already been through a lot simply for the sin of losing her heart to the wrong asshole. She's fragile and halfway broken. I'm warning you now… Don't you *dare* fucking take advantage of her."

Whoa. "I'm a professional, Mr. Lund. My job is to protect her body, not to ravish it or whatever."

No matter how much I'd like to.

On the other side of the room, Amanda gapes, then storms back in my direction and sticks out her hand, lips pressed together mulishly.

"Your sister has something to say," I drawl and hand the device back to her.

This ought to be entertaining.

"Knock it off, Stephen!" she hisses. "Tanner is trying to *help* me, and you're being an ass." She pauses to listen, then her eyes widen with fresh fury. "Stop acting like I can't be trusted alone with a man. This is a very different situation than…well, you know." Another breather where she's presumably listening again. "What are you saying? That you think I spread my legs for every guy? One. That's my 'number.' What's yours, big brother?"

Is she saying she's only ever had sex with Barclay Reed?

At Stephen's reply, she grips the phone, jaw clenched. "Fine." She looks my way. "How old are you?"

Why does it matter? "Thirty-eight."

I'll be thirty-nine in less than two months, but I doubt that factoid will make the conversation more productive.

"Thank you," she says to me, then turns and speaks into the device again. "I'm sure you heard he's not even forty, so take your judgmental crack about me being attracted to guys nearly Social Security eligible and shove it."

She jerks her gaze away, but not before I see her cheeks turn red. And her eyes fill with tears.

That's it. I don't care what these people can do to me for sticking my nose in their family business. I'm going to tear this guy a new asshole.

I cross the room to her and hold out my hand. "Let me talk to your brother again."

"It's not your problem."

"The minute I took this job, it became my problem."

Her sigh sounds defeated. "It won't change anything."

The fuck it won't. I motion with my fingers at her to give the device over. "Hand me the phone."

With a shrug, she puts it in my hand. "Don't say I didn't warn you."

The second the device makes contact with my palm, I point to the spot where she stands. "Stay here." Then I plaster the device against my ear, head out to Joe's balcony, then shut the door behind me as the warm Hawaiian breeze hits my face. "Listen, I don't know what the fuck is up with you, but your sister has been through a lot in the last few hours. If you actually care about her, you could try backing the hell off and—"

"My sister has been through a lot for the last two years, but she *chose* to get involved with Barclay Reed."

Maybe so, but... "If you were so bent up about it, why didn't you stop it?"

"Because I didn't know it was going on until it was too late. I was based out of New York, and Amanda moved to LA. But even if I'd been there, I doubt I could have stopped her. She'd had a serious case of hero worship for that lying bastard since she was a teenager. She was so excited to work for him. When I found out about their affair, I wasn't terribly surprised since she has daddy issues."

"Do you think that just because she was attracted to someone older?"

"Why else would she have looked to a man old enough to be her father for approval and affection? Why else was she anxious when she didn't hear from Reed frequently? Then again, he gave her more than one reason to feel insecure." Before I can ask what he means, Stephen goes on. "But she has a son now, and it's been almost two years since Reed dumped her. The time has come for some tough love. How else will she figure out why she looked to a womanizer Reed's age so she can knock it the fuck off? You insisting on being alone with her isn't going to help."

God, he annoys me. "First, I'm not old enough to be her father. Second, I'm sure when she got involved with Reed she never imagined she'd be dealing with angry mobs threatening her life. And third, if she's seeking something emotionally to find happiness, then who the hell are you to question what she needs? Clearly, Reed wasn't the right guy, but just because you disapprove doesn't make her wrong. I admit that I only met your sister a few hours ago, but I know she needs your support now, not your scorn. If you can't manage that, then why don't you fuck off while I help her solve this problem?"

"You know what? If you manage to make her problems disappear, I can almost guarantee she'll develop a case of hero worship for you, too, and latch on tight. I don't think you want that." He pauses, and I can almost hear his thoughts turning. "Unless you're already hot to fuck her."

"If I am, you're the last person I'll admit that to. But even if Reed may have seen her as a piece of ass—"

"He saw every woman as a piece of ass. My sister is just one in a long line of executive assistants he knocked up."

Did Amanda know that when she went to work for him? Surely not. Despite Stephen's claims that his sister is looking for a daddy to save her, she seems to have plenty of gumption without a man in her life.

"Like Evan Cook's mother?"

"She was one, yes. Reed had three illegitimate children—that we know of. We're all betting there are more."

"He sounds like a real peach, but I'm nothing like him. My job is to make sure your sister stays safe. Nothing is more important to me right now."

"How is she paying you? She drained what little savings she had trying to pay lawyers and take care of Oliver."

"Unless you'd like to pay me, I don't think that's any of your business. She and I will work it out." Hopefully. I should be concerned that she might be broke, but right now I'm more annoyed that her brother won't back off.

"So you haven't talked money yet?" His tone suggests he doesn't think I'm very smart for letting that slide.

"Getting her to a location where the crazy mob couldn't find her was a tad more important in the moment. Or did you want me to stand out in the open with her where any murderer could end her while we worked out a payment plan?"

"Your sarcasm isn't helpful."

"Your assholery isn't, either."

He grunts, but that's an improvement over the blow-up I expected. "I want to talk to my sister again."

I turn to peek through the glass of the door to find Amanda staring out the window of the parking lot. She stands unmoving, brittle, chin lifted. Beautiful...but so damn sad. A tear rolls down her cheek.

Why does that fucking bother me?

"She's not up for that right now since you made her cry. Maybe when she's done sobbing she'll feel like talking to you, but—"

"She's crying?" He huffs. "Fuck."

"You were an absolute bastard. What did you expect?"

"I didn't mean to upset her. It's just... The last twenty-four hours have been a bitch. I've been worried I'm going to lose my unborn baby. Now I'm terrified for my little sister. I haven't slept. I haven't eaten. My anxiety level is..."

Huge, I get it. But he's trying to excuse his behavior to me, and I'm not buying it. "You've got a lot going on. Worry about your wife. Make sure she keeps that baby. I'll focus on Amanda. When we get settled, I'll text you my number. You can contact me for status updates. But I've got this. I'll neutralize the threat so she can live another day and figure out what she's looking for in life and why."

"And what if she decides she wants you to be her next 'daddy'?"

We're both adults, and that would be between us. "If you can keep your snark to yourself, you can talk to her. If not, fuck off."

"You're already taking care of her. You realize that, don't you?"

I grimace because he's right. This is the "overbearing" side of me that Ellie despised. "What's it going to be?"

He sighs. "I want to talk to her one more time."

"If she starts crying again, you're done."

"She's already got you wrapped around her finger, doesn't she?" Stephen laughs. "Oh, buddy... You're fucked."

Chapter Three

I refuse to justify Stephen's shit with a reply. Instead, I push the balcony door open. Amanda whirls to me.

"He wants to talk to you again." I hold the phone in her direction. "Are you up for it?"

Reluctantly, she nods. Over the next few minutes, Amanda and her brother manage to have a mostly civil conversation. I do my best not to eavesdrop as I pack, but even if I can't hear Stephen's words, it's impossible to miss his persuasive tone. She darts quick glances in my direction and answers in monosyllables.

They're talking about me. Nifty. I don't care as long as he's not taking swipes at Amanda and she's not crying.

Finally, she hangs up and pockets her phone, then turns to me with a frown. "What did you say to him?"

I can't tell whether she's angry or shocked. "What I needed to so he'd back the hell off."

Amanda cocks her head. "Stephen has a strong personality, and most people cave when he confronts them. Thank you."

She's happy? "You're welcome."

"I'm sorry you found yourself in the middle of our argument."

Butted in, more like. I shouldn't have. And I don't want to question why seeing her upset bothered me so much. "It's fine." I toss the last few items into my duffel, then pick up my gun case and turn to her again. "I'll be right back."

As soon as I secure my luggage in the trunk next to hers, I scan the parking lot, looking for trouble. Thankfully, I don't see any—yet. But it's coming. I feel it.

After a quick duck inside, I see Amanda sitting on the edge of the bed, ruffling her sleeping son's hair. "What do we do now?"

"Find a place to lie low. I'm hoping Trace comes through with a location soon. I've barely been on the island for a week, and you've been here even less…"

"Other than my drive from the airport and lunch in town yesterday, I haven't seen much. Sorry I'm not more helpful."

"We'll figure something out." I try to sound as if I'm not worried, but I am. We need to get out of limbo and into hiding before her knife-wielding asshole tracks her down again.

"How did you and Trace meet?"

She's making small talk, and I don't mind. "Joe, the guy who's apartment I'm crashing in, left me a list of places and activities I might like before he left the island on business. He's hired Trace in the past for some fishing excursions, so I did the same shortly after I arrived. We hit it off, and we've gone out for a beer or two since then. He's a good guy." I shrug. "You and Nia seem close."

"We're working on it. The truth is, I didn't even know she existed until last November. I knew my dad and our maid had a fling after things between him and my mom fell apart, but that all happened before I was born. Then Stephen and my dad walked into a meeting last November to negotiate a deal with Evan Cook and met Nia, who was his assistant then. About a month later, Stephen told Nia we all share the same father. Until then, she had no idea. At the time, I was too wrapped up with Oliver. After he was born, I really struggled."

"Difficult birth?"

"Thankfully no. I just wasn't sure what to do with my life. Barclay made it clear he wasn't interested in me or our child, and I had no job since he'd fired me."

"What a bastard." How or why did she ever think she loved him? She'd been young and probably naive—two things a player like him would relish. Then he'd likely used his position of power to seduce Amanda because she'd been vulnerable. Had she let him because she was really looking for some sort of father figure? Does she still like the idea of an older man being her "daddy"?

I need to hop off this dangerous train of thought.

"Yes, but I…" She shakes her head. "It doesn't matter; I was wrong. Then he got arrested, and the press went insane. I tried to get a new job, but no one wanted to hire an assistant who came with so much baggage. Inevitably I ran out of money, and I had to start making hard choices. I had every reason to leave LA, but Stephen helped me financially until I reached the end of my lease. I'm sure that's why he thinks he can stick his nose in my business. Well, and he's my big brother. But I just want to start over clean. That's why I came to Hawaii. I've spoken to Nia over the phone for the last couple of months, and she invited me to stay with her until I got settled somewhere. But clearly I can't. I'm doubting a fresh start is even possible. But don't worry about the money. I'll make sure you get paid."

"We can talk about that later." Sure, I need the cash, but she's got a full plate, along with a smorgasbord of problems. I can be patient.

Silence falls, stretching out long and uncomfortably. I reach for my phone.

Maybe I should call the coffee shop I tried the other day. The owner said a lot of active and retired cops frequent his place. It's possible one of them would be better suited to protect Amanda after our week is up. But I've never met any of them. Would someone else really ensure her safety—without taking advantage of her?

I pocket my phone again. Sure, I might like looking at Amanda, but nothing will ever happen between us. She's ass-deep in problems, and I'm at the tail end of a divorce. Neither of us needs entanglements. But I can keep her safe; I know that. Despite everything, she's better off with me.

I'm spared the awkwardness between us—most of it because I can't stop mentally undressing Amanda—when my phone rings. I pluck it free again and read the display with relief. "Trace. Talk to me."

"I found a place. Amanda can stay there at least another ten days. If no one has found her by then, there's an option to extend her stay another two weeks." He tells me it's a vacation villa right on the Pacific in a gated community. The neighborhood is exclusive and quiet, the beach damn near private. It's got four bedrooms, three bathrooms. And best of all, Amanda and I can move in this morning. "My…um, friend, Masey, rented it for her vacation, but she's willing to come crash with me so you two can have it. Come on by so we can give you a tour."

"That sounds great." Perfect, in fact. "How soon can we meet you?"

After we negotiate a time, he ends the call and texts me the address. I glance at my watch.

"Trace found somewhere?" she asks.

"Looks like. We've got a while before they'll arrive. You haven't eaten. Neither have I. If we leave now, we can grab something on the way."

She glances reluctantly at Oliver. Whatever her faults or sins, she loves her son and would do anything for him. I admire that about her. I can't not look at her with lust, and I'd be lying if I said she didn't intrigue me. I want to see the vulnerable woman I first glimpsed, now hidden behind her icy wall, open to me. I want to understand how she came to this point in life. More than anything, I feel compelled to protect her.

"Yeah." She sighs. "We all need to eat. If Oliver doesn't soon, he'll get cranky."

"You need me to carry him back to the car?"

She looks up at me, those blue eyes somewhere between surprised and grateful. "I would really appreciate that."

It's a small task that requires almost no effort, but I suspect the men in her life haven't been kind to her. Why? She's made mistakes, sure. But she's paying for them. And unless something changes, she'll be paying for them for years to come.

"No problem." I scan the little apartment to ensure I've packed up all my gear. I toss out the rest of last night's takeout. Joe will appreciate the beer I'm leaving behind. The bedroom and bathroom are about as clean as he left them. I take a minute to jot him a note thanking him and let him know I'll run his spare key back as soon as I'm able. "Let's go."

Without thinking, I hold out my hand to her. She looks at it, then up at me. "You're not mad anymore?"

"I was never mad."

"You were. At Nia's house."

"No. I was concerned. An intruder is serious."

"I know." She looks away. "I've never been more terrified in my life."

And I yelled. She must think I'm an ass. "You were very brave, and you protected your son. You did well."

She shakes her head. "I got lucky. He tripped in the dark. While he was trying to regain his balance, I kneed him—hard. I was panicked. I screamed and kicked and hit him over the head with a vase."

"Which tells me you'll have the guts to defend yourself even more successfully once I teach you some moves."

"I tried. I wanted to put him down so the police could arrest him when they came. Even though he bled, like, a lot, the guy got away. The officers who investigated looked at the pool of blood and scolded me for using excessive force."

Is she serious? "Those officers were idiots. You did what you had to, and I'm glad you didn't hold back."

The corners of her lush mouth curl up in a mysterious Mona-Lisa smile. Amanda is beautiful—no question—but that expression takes my fucking breath away.

Bodyguarding her could be decidedly tricky.

Still, I sense almost no one has been in her corner since she got pregnant. I hate to turn my back on her, too. I just need to ignore my sexual urges. I've managed to do that for the past few months. What's another week?

But you've never encountered a temptation like her.

Trying to ignore that inconvenient truth, I extend my hand to her again. "You ready to head out now?"

When she slides her hand into mine, the sizzle streaking up my arm isn't new...but it's annoyingly stronger. Worse, I have absolutely no control. I'm hyperaware of her softness, her faintly floral scent, and the ping of her gaze at me when her blue eyes fasten on mine.

"Um...sure." She rises to her feet. "I should get Oliver fed and down for his usual morning nap."

I clear my throat and force myself to release her. "What about you?"

"I'll nap when he naps."

My eyes narrow as I stare at her. "How much did you sleep last night?"

"About two hours. I've survived on less. I'll be fine."

"No, you need more than a scattered nap or two. You need to be rested and alert, especially in case you need to defend yourself."

"Well, a twelve-month-old can't exactly be left to his own devices. Are *you* going to babysit him?" she asks, pale brow raised in challenge.

"If I need to."

"Absolutely not."

This argument is going nowhere. She might hate me being as "overbearing" as my ex-wife, but Amanda isn't calling the shots while her safety is on the line.

"Let's go." I nudge her toward the door.

If I don't, if I stand here with her face under mine, with her lush mouth just inches away, I'll keep thinking things I shouldn't. I'll stop remembering that doing them isn't smart and start wondering if doing them is possible. I might even convince myself she wants me to.

Don't be a dumb ass. Step back, pick up the kid, and act like a professional.

Scooping up Oliver, I peek out the door and scan the parking lot. I still don't see anyone. There's a couple with two little kids walking toward the beach a block away. I see an old guy drinking his morning coffee on his balcony across the street. A pair of women are talking a few yards down as one's antsy dog runs in circles on its leash. I can't be one hundred percent certain that none of them pose a threat, but my senses tell me they mean Amanda no harm.

I step aside and let her ease out the door. Her body brushes me as she passes, and I wish I wasn't so aware of her.

"Wait." I block those nearby from spotting her with my body as I lock the door, escort her to the car, then hastily set Oliver in his car seat.

She taps me on the shoulder. "Do you need help?"

I could probably figure out the buckles and straps of this contraption eventually, but I'd hate to do something wrong in my ignorance. "Sure."

As I step back, she leans in. I try not to leer at her ass. Or any of her, really. Ellie did her best to enlighten me, and I understand how unwarranted staring could be unwelcome. Besides, Amanda isn't looking for a lover. And when I'm with her, I shouldn't be, either.

Moments later, she straightens. I escort her to the passenger's side and open the door. I'm not sure what reaction I expected. I didn't foresee her eyes zipping up to mine.

"Trying to be a gentleman?"

I'd suspect she was being snide if her face didn't seem so wary. "No. My ex-wife hated gestures like this. But there are seven visible people nearby, any of whom could see you if I wasn't blocking their view."

She tries to peek around my shoulder. "I only saw the family heading to the beach. Who else?"

I grasp her face and hold her in place. "There are others. You're going to have to trust me on this or we don't have any business continuing this arrangement."

"Fine." She stops trying to peep behind me and slides into the car.

I shut the door and slip into the driver's seat. When I turn the Mustang over, the engine roars. "What do you want for breakfast?"

We settle on donuts because Oliver isn't awake yet, and his food would only get cold before he ate it. When we pull away from the drive-through, I notice she only drinks her coffee.

GPS tells me we have twelve minutes before we arrive at Trace's location. I turned off the music as soon as I started up the car since it's obvious we're not going to agree on tunes. And as we stop at a light, Amanda glances out her window at the row of houses beyond a tall fence.

The golden sun illuminates her profile and makes her all but glow. I shift in my seat, but there's no ignoring her effect on me.

"Would five thousand be enough to make you stay for the week?" she asks suddenly.

That's more than I expected. It would certainly help me secure a lease and start acquiring equipment I need to open my doors. But we have to be real. "Do you really have that kind of money?"

"Now? No. But I can get it in a couple of days. If I promised you that, would you stay a whole week?"

Grilling her doesn't seem right after the night she's had. Besides, I'm dangerously reluctant to leave her side. "Yeah."

"Would you stay another week for an additional five thousand?"

"Let's see if you even need me beyond a few days. You may decide that you're safer after some firearms and self-defense training, then use that money to find another high-security building like you had in LA. That would solve a lot of your problems."

"Maybe." But she doesn't sound convinced.

What is she not telling me? I can't begin to guess, but there's something...

Silence descends again, barely punctuated by the rev of the classic car's engine and the robotic directions my GPS gives. Finally, we turn onto a street cordoned off by an electronic gate. After I punch in the code Trace texted me, I zoom toward a shimmering white villa situated on a picturesque beach. This place is a giant step up from Joe's apartment.

My occasional beer-drinking buddy ducks out the front door and waves my way as I pull up to the curb.

I turn to Amanda to gage her reaction. She doesn't seem to have one, but she looks both taut and tired, like she can't decide whether she'll crack or needs to escape into the numbness of slumber. "You okay?"

"Fine."

In my experience, when a woman says she's fine, she never is. But I'm betting Amanda won't appreciate me using the lessons I learned during marriage on her. I swallow a curse. "I'll get Oliver."

"Thanks." Her gaze barely skims me.

I climb out of the car, then lean in to pluck up the boy. He takes one look at me with bleary, half-open eyes, then starts to wail.

Fuck, what did I do wrong?

Trace rushes over. "Need help?"

"Pointers, maybe. I've never been around kids."

"Ever?"

"Nope. I'm an only child. But more importantly, I need my hands free…just in case." Someone violent is lying in wait.

Trace nods like he understands. "Masey and I have been here for a bit. We haven't seen anyone."

"Great." But that doesn't mean the place is safe. It may mean that whoever's after Amanda is just good.

She climbs out of the car and dashes around to claim Oliver, cradling him protectively as she shoots me an apologetic glance. "Sorry. He's still behind on his sleep."

Does she think I'm going to be angry because he's fussy? "It's no problem."

She sends me a stilted smile, then turns to my buddy. "Hi, Trace. Do you know where I can lay my son down?"

"I don't. I've only been here a few minutes, but my friend, Masey, is inside. Since she knows her way around this place, she'll help you."

"Thanks." She grabs her diaper bag from inside the muscle car, soothes her fussy son with a soft whisper, then shoots me a sidelong stare before she disappears inside.

"How's that going?" he asks.

I watch Amanda walk toward the house. Every instinct I possess tells me to stay on her ass—not just the bodyguard in me…but the man. The latter is the only reason I'm giving her an inch of space. "Um…interesting."

"That doesn't sound good. Shit. Sorry, man. I'll pay you for your time and headache."

"No." I appreciate the offer, but I don't want Amanda beholden to him in any way. My instinct is stupidly possessive; I think he's got something going on with whoever Masey is. But I still don't want him between Amanda and me. "She's got it. We've worked something out."

He frowns. "But?"

I'm not surprised he's sensed the undercurrent between us. "She's wary."

"Of you?"

"Until now, I didn't know if it was me or men in general. But she doesn't have a problem with you." And that chaps me.

"What do you think is going on?"

"I have some theories."

Mostly that she's attracted to me, too. She's definitely looked. God knows I have. It's a bad idea all the way around.

Trace nods. "Got any luggage?"

"Yeah. I could use a hand."

He hauls my duffel and Oliver's rolling suitcase with the race-car motif inside. I handle Amanda's enormous bag and my gun case.

The inside of the house is huge and airy, everything seemingly neutral and white. I follow the sounds of women chatting softly, bypassing one suitcase in the middle of the hall, and find them in the master bedroom with a wall of windows open to the morning sun and one-hundred-eighty-degree ocean views. Like the rest of the house, neutrals and whites make a muted statement, letting the paradise all around shout its color and beauty.

This place must have cost a fortune to rent. I won't mind staying here for a week.

I haul Amanda's bag into the corner and spot her and a pretty, petite brunette, who I presume is Masey, talking in the spacious bathroom. Both look through the wide, open arch to the spacious closet, where I see Oliver already stretched out on the floor, surrounded by pillows. I guess that will do until the crib arrives.

"Need anything else?" the brunette asks Amanda.

"Did you find a grocery store nearby? Or a delivery service?"

Masey fills her in on both. Trace introduces me to her before he starts hauling boxes out of what looks like an office space next to the master while his infant son babbles and shakes a soft toy from his bouncy seat in the corner.

On his way back in, I snag his attention. "Hey, man. Where did you stash my bag?"

I'd like to set my gun case down and begin to settle in. I definitely need to tour the place, assess its strengths and weaknesses, make any adjustments necessary for safety before night falls.

"Living room. I didn't know where you'd want it. The spare bedrooms are on the other end of the house." He thumbs in the opposite direction from the master.

That's too far away from Amanda when she's at her most vulnerable...but sleeping in the same room with her would be a bad,

bad idea. "I'll crash on the floor of that room next to hers."

"Sure. If you need anything else, let me know. Griff and Britta said they'd be by after lunch to drop off the crib."

Having anyone know our location isn't optimal, but they have a crib and I don't have a damn vehicle big enough to cart it. "Thanks. And thank Masey for giving us a safe place to crash. It's above and beyond."

He sends me a sly grin as he lifts another box. "I'll make sure she doesn't regret staying with me."

Masey follows him out the door when a roadside assistance truck arrives to change a flat tire on Trace's truck. His baby boy, Ranger, seems to have drifted off. Still not a peep from Oliver in the master closet.

But where the hell is Amanda? I tear through the house. She's not in the master or the office beside it. She's not in the living room, the expansive kitchen, or either of the spare bedrooms on the far side of the house. Alarm sets in after I scan the laundry room. She's not in the garage, either.

My alarm turns to panic when I realize I've searched the entire house. It's empty. Amanda is gone.

Fuck!

I stick my head out the front door. Trace, Masey, and a roadside assistance guy are all hovered around his truck as a flat comes off and the spare fits on. No Amanda there. I scan the house again, running from room to room—kitchen, laundry room, living room, office— shouting her name. At this point, I don't give a shit if the little ones wake up. I need to find her.

My heart revs. Terrible possibilities start pelting my brain. Did someone follow us? Wait for the first moment I was distracted to seize her and drag her away against her will? Is she, even now, fighting off the asshole with the knife, struggling for her life?

"Amanda!"

Panic burns through my veins as I again see a still-sleeping Ranger in the office and Oliver undisturbed in the master closet. I try to remind myself that Amanda has fended off this guy before. She may be small, but she's strong-willed. She'll fight for herself. She'll fight for her son.

But with me here, she shouldn't have to, much less alone.

"Amanda!" I tear out of the master again and charge toward the hall. "Amanda!"

"What?" I hear her just before I round the corner. I find her standing in the middle of the hall, staring at me like she has no idea why I'm overreacting.

Multiple reactions hit me at once. Relief. Of course I'm thanking God she's okay, but I'm still confused. Anger hits next, and I march straight for her. I'm damn near seething when I shove her against the nearest wall and pin her to it, planting my palm over her head. "Where the fuck did you go?"

"Out back. To see the beach."

Is she kidding me? "Alone? Without telling me where you were off to?"

"I-I…" She doesn't finish her sentence, but I see understanding cross her face.

"Didn't think?"

"I'm not used to answering to anyone."

"Get used to it."

"Look, I hired you to keep me safe, not to be my—" She bites her lip like she knows better than to finish that sentence.

"Daddy?" I lean closer. Our eyes lock. "Is that what you were going to say?"

The air between us turns thick. I see her breasts rising and falling inches from my chest. Her rough breaths are audible. Her eyes dilate.

Do I scare her? Or is she aware that I'm not just a bodyguard, but a man?

Amanda raises her chin. "You're not."

It takes all my willpower not to touch her. "If you're going to wander off alone when someone is out to kill you, I have no problem being yours."

Footsteps stomp through the front door moments before Trace and Masey round the corner and spot us. I jerk back. Amanda looks away in embarrassment.

Trace clears his throat. "We just…um, need to grab Ranger and his gear from the office."

"Sure." I gesture him to the room at the end of the hall. I'm trying my damnedest not to look guilty, but I feel the thick sludge rolling through me, pushing the flash of anger from my veins.

Amanda didn't need me to yell at her. We haven't had time to cover ground rules and best practices. That didn't stop me from jumping down her throat.

Maybe Ellie wasn't all wrong about you being overprotective and possessive.

But this is worse. Way worse. Stronger. Maybe I'm just on edge—I hope that's it—but not knowing that Amanda was safe did something to more than my temper.

Trace and Masey step past us and disappear into the office. An instant later, Amanda backs away from me, putting distance between us.

"I think I'll just…get some water." She whirls for the kitchen as if her ass is on fire.

It takes everything I have not to follow.

The silence is awkward as Trace and Masey emerge with Ranger, then disappear with a few mumbled words, closing the door behind them with a final click.

I let out a breath and scowl. I've botched everything, and I need to apologize.

On my way down the hall, I pass the front door, ensure it's locked, then do the same with the double glass doors in the back overlooking the Pacific. Finally, I take a deep breath and get my shit under control before I head into the kitchen to see Amanda facing the sink, staring out the window. The glass in her hand is shaking.

I feel like a shit. "I'm sorry."

She gives me a tight shake of her head. "You're here to protect me, and I…wanted to see the ocean."

Her explanation makes sense, but her hesitation as she voices her excuse tells me she's lying. "I don't believe you."

That makes her turn and look my way. She sets her glass on the pristine white counter. "I have a lot on my mind."

We're getting closer to the truth, I sense. But that's not everything. "Any of that have to do with me?"

"Why are you here?"

"For the money."

"If that's the case, why won't you stay on the job beyond a week?" Her gaze drills me. "I suggested a sum that should have been more than acceptable. You didn't even consider it. As long as you lie to me, I won't feel bad about lying to you."

Damn it. Every time I fall into the trap of thinking she's soft and vulnerable, she proves she's made of stronger stuff. "I'm not lying; I need the money. But I also came because I don't like women or children being threatened."

"I'm not asking the right questions. Why were you worried about me just now? Honestly."

What is she pushing me for? "It would be better if I didn't answer that. Once I tell you, you can't unknow it."

Our gazes connect, and electricity pings between us. Goose bumps flare across my skin. Desire kindles in my gut.

Her whisper is the match that sets me ablaze. "You want me."

I could try to lie, but it won't work. Amanda knows. The elephant is in the middle of the room. "I've already thought about stripping you naked and fucking you until you scream about a hundred times."

She's going to fire me now. I haven't just crossed a line; I've stomped over it, backed up, and rolled over it a few more times for good measure. I deserve for her to show me the exit, slam the door behind me, and yell "good riddance."

The last thing I expect is for her to lick her lips and glance my way. "And I've already thought a hundred times about letting you."

Oh, holy shit.

I scrub my hand across my face. How the fuck am I going to stay off of her now that I know what I'm craving is mutual? "You went outside to put distance between us?"

She nods. "I needed to. We both know giving in to this would be a terrible idea."

"The worst."

"Beyond stupid."

"Catastrophic."

But that doesn't stop me from prowling closer. Amanda steps back. I need to respect the distance she's putting between us. I shouldn't follow her. But I can't stop myself from lunging into her personal space. She edges away again, until the counter at her back stops her.

She has nowhere else to go.

A smile that isn't comforting curls across my face. "All you have to do is tell me to back off."

"Why should I have to? You should give me space, regardless."

Her trembling voice does something to me. Not because she's afraid. I know she's not. Because that, along with her darting gaze, tells me my nearness affects her.

"I should, but I still want to hear you say it—and mean it."

Amanda presses her lips together, refusing to say anything at all.

Thrill spikes through my blood. I shuffle closer until our chests brush. Until I see her pulse beating frantically at her neck. Until I feel her choppy breaths on my lips.

I lean forward and brace my hands on the counter on either side of her hips. "Nothing to say?"

"I'd rather not lie."

Fuck, her pouty pink lips are less than a whisper away, and it takes all my self-control not to fasten my mouth over hers and eat her whole. "It's a good thing you didn't. What the hell are we going to do stuck together for a whole week?"

"Be adults and ignore it." Amanda nudges me aside and tries to walk away.

I should let her. But the devil in me won't let it go.

I grab her arm and yank her back to me. "Is that really what you want?"

Chapter Four

"My last relationship taught me to stop thinking about what I want and start thinking about what I need."

She means Barclay. What did that bastard do to her?

Yeah, Amanda has only asked me to be her bodyguard, and I should leave it there. I shouldn't care about her broken heart or the way she's barricaded it against me. But I do. And I have a feeling that I need to understand exactly what happened between her and her lover thirty-three years her senior to understand her. Unfortunately, there's no way in hell she's ready to tell me now.

No matter how much it chafes, I need to be patient.

I watch her go as she disappears into the master bedroom, shutting the door between us. The pipes and pelting water tell me she's taking a shower. Soon afterward, I hear the whir of mechanical blinds descending. Then silence. I use the opportunity to locate an inflatable mattress in the hall closet and situate it in the office beside the master. I make sure my firearms are both ready and up high where Oliver can never reach them. I text Stephen Lund my number so he can talk to me about his sister, then sit down to start an online grocery order.

Not three minutes later, my phone rings. I don't recognize the number, but it has a 212 prefix. New York. I'd bet a hundred bucks that Stephen didn't like what he heard from me earlier, so he ran his displeasure up the family flagpole. Now Lund Senior is probably ringing to ream me out.

"Tanner Kirk."

"Douglas Lund here."

The guy sounds commanding. Rich and powerful. Like someone I shouldn't fuck with.

How on earth did he let a dirty old man, even a supposed friend like Barclay Reed, debauch his daughter?

"What can I do for you, sir?"

Now comes the part where he growls and warns me away from Amanda. Probably threatens me, too.

"Is Amanda nearby?"

"Sleeping. After the intruder last night, she didn't get much rest." I hope like hell he doesn't ask me to wake her.

"Good. I want to talk to you."

That isn't an encouraging sign, either. "I'm listening. I know you must be worried about your daughter—"

"Very much."

"I know your son and I had a…contentious conversation this morning—"

"Stephen doesn't always focus on what's important. Do I wish I knew you and your reputation better? Of course. Am I more worried about my daughter's virtue than her safety? No."

"I assure you she's in good hands. I've been a bodyguard for more than one Colorado State senator and even the former governor for a spell." I don't mention that was nearly fifteen years ago. "I'm damn good with a gun, and I'll do whatever it takes to make sure Amanda and Oliver stay safe."

"How much has she offered to pay you?"

"Five thousand for this week. That's as long as I can stay. She'll be looking to replace me after that."

"I see," he drawls, and behind those words I sense he's gearing up for something more… "Tanner. Can I call you that?"

"Sure." I don't give a fuck. I just want to know what he's after.

"It didn't take me five minutes to dig into you. I know you ran a successful gun range once upon a time, which you had to sell to pay off your soon-to-be ex-wife after you filed for divorce. I know you're nearly thirty-nine, broke, and don't have a place to live. I'm guessing you took this job because you don't know where to go or what to do with your life next."

He's mischaracterizing me—and rubbing me the wrong way. "What's your point?"

"Amanda doesn't have a dime to her name right now. She thinks she'll simply cajole me later into paying your fee, and I'll assure her I will. But how much you make from your time with her is up to you."

My gut tightens. "I don't follow."

"Amanda doesn't belong in Hawaii with my illegitimate daughter and all my former friend's offspring. I need to do what I should have after she graduated college, and that's help her find the right future."

"Why didn't you get involved then?" I can't keep the accusation out of my tone.

"It's a fair question, especially since it seems you're looking after her." He tries to sound reasonable.

I'm not buying it. "I am."

"To be honest, I thought she was a grown woman. She had a college degree in hand and she'd always been a good girl. Stayed out of trouble. Rarely dated. Never partied. Never gave me any reason to suspect she lacked the common sense needed to sidestep Barclay Reed's womanizing ways. As such, when she graduated, I let her adult. It was a regrettable mistake on my part since all hell broke loose."

I understand his perspective. Who wouldn't think their college graduate able to handle their office job and their love life when they'd never shown any hint of being inept or reckless? But I don't agree with his notion that Amanda making choices he doesn't approve of gives him carte blanche to control her life. She was, after all, an adult. It was her life to ruin.

"What are you proposing?"

"There's a man here in New York, one she's known since they were kids. Son of a good family. Bruce has been in love with Amanda since, well, probably puberty. He'll marry her tomorrow and take care of Oliver, too. All she has to do is say yes and come home."

It may be that simple in his eyes, but there's a reason Amanda isn't with Bruce now. "How does she feel about him?"

"You know how women can be. Stubborn mules with lipstick." He laughs, but it's forced.

I'm offended on women's behalf, especially Amanda's. She's stubborn, but not without reason. And she certainly isn't a fucking mule.

"Anyway," Lund goes on. "She hasn't given Bruce a fair shake. She's always considered him more like an older brother. When they were teenagers, that was great. But she's twenty-six now and a mother. He's thirtyish and worth half a billion dollars. He's prepared to take care of her. She just needs the right incentive to let him."

"So what is it you want me to do?"

"I'll pay you fifty thousand dollars if you'll let Bruce visit her there in Maui so he can convince her to come home and get respectably married. There's an extra ten grand in it for you if she agrees to his proposal in the next three days."

Is he crazy? "With all due respect, sir, I don't think—"

"Do us both a favor and save the speech. This is one time you shouldn't think with your morals, son. Think with your wallet."

I grip my phone, bristling. "I'm not your son, and I'd appreciate you not telling me how to think."

He gives me the forced laugh again. "You misunderstand. Figure of speech."

"Amanda's future should be her decision."

"Well, you see how good her decisions are when she's left to her own devices. It's come to my attention that she looked to Barclay Reed to be her 'daddy' because I didn't pay enough attention to her as a kid or something like that."

"That's Stephen's theory." Personally, I think Amanda has felt alone and overwhelmed, so she's been looking for a partner, not someone to give her milk and braid her hair.

"Maybe he's right. I was busy with work, and resented the hell out of her mother for tricking me into getting pregnant as an insurance policy against divorce. But none of that was Amanda's fault, and if I didn't give her the guidance she needed as a child, rest assured I will now."

I swallow back the less-than-kind observation that it's too late for Amanda's father to play daddy. She's already looked beyond him. And if Stephen is right, if she's genuinely seeking a father figure to protect her and share her load, I see two choices: either I let Bruce come in and do it—which makes me want to punch my fist into the nearest wall. Or I do it myself.

They're both fucking bad ideas. What do I have to offer Amanda?

"I don't think she's interested in anyone forcing their guidance on her. Your daughter is very strong-willed."

"She is," he agrees. "But my will is stronger. Once she talks to Bruce, I think she'll understand he's where her future lies."

I think he's full of shit, and I'm pissed on her behalf. "No."

"No, you don't agree?"

"No, I won't tell you where to find us. It's a dangerous, potentially fatal risk simply so Bruce can drag her home like a naughty little girl."

"Let's be honest. She's behaved like one."

Does he realize how condescending he's being? "I think she's finding her way in the world. We all make mistakes when we're younger, then correct course."

"She made more than a mistake. She stepped in a steaming pile of shit. I'm giving her a handout now. An easy way out of her mess. All she has to do is say 'I do' to someone she already likes and trusts."

"I can't stop her if she wants to marry Bruce, but she hired me to protect her. I'm going to do that until she tells me otherwise."

"Seventy-five thousand, with a fifteen thousand dollar bonus if she agrees by Thursday to come home with Bruce."

"It's a generous offer, but I don't have any sway over her. We just met this morning."

"Stephen seems to think otherwise, just like he thinks you're eager to get her into bed."

I can hardly call him a liar when it's true. "The answer is still no."

"It's admirable of you to defend not just her privacy, but her character. Tell you what, a hundred thousand, with a twenty-five K bonus if she's on a plane wearing Bruce's engagement ring by Friday."

I need the money so fucking bad. That would set my business up for at least a year and allow me to buy a condo now. Those are just two of many reasons to say yes. I only have one reason to refuse him, and that's Amanda. "No."

"You're loyal. Good trait in a man. I admire that."

"Don't butter me up."

"Maybe I wasn't plain earlier, Tanner. If you don't help me steer Amanda toward the right future, you'll walk away empty-handed. I won't pay you a dime for protecting her this week. Then how will you put a roof over your head? It's expensive in Maui, and you can't afford the plane ticket home, son."

"I'm *not* your son."

"Just tell me where to find Amanda and talk Bruce up, and you won't have to worry about money for a long while."

I hesitate. He makes a good point. Where the hell will I be at the end of a week? A couple hundred bucks poorer and without a place to hang my hat. Even if my house sells tomorrow, escrow won't close for at least thirty days, maybe more. The guy who owns the building where I'd like to open the shooting range told me when I toured the facility that I wasn't the only one looking at it.

Fuck.

"I'll think about it and let you know tomorrow."

Douglas Lund hesitates, and I can almost feel his frustration through the phone, but he gives me more forced affability. "Sure. Tomorrow. Best make it early if you want that bonus. Bruce is just waiting to sweep Amanda off her feet and snap her up as his wife."

A trio of beeps in my ear tells me Lund hung up. I resist the urge—barely—to slam my phone on the counter. If I did, I'd only break it and I can't afford to replace it.

"Ma ma!" A teary Oliver cries down the hall, bottom lip quivering, as he drags a blue cotton blanket with trains and stars behind him.

I dash the boy's way and kneel in front of him. I know zero about children, but I know a lot about women. Amanda needs sleep. "You want donuts?"

It's afternoon, but this is the first chance he's had to eat.

The boy scowls and looks like he's ready to open his mouth and wail again, so I pluck him off his feet, hustle him to the kitchen, then set him down on the counter. I drag the little carton of milk she bought at the donut shop out of the fridge, plow through the bag of donuts, then set both in front of him. "Hungry?"

Quickly, he reaches out one little hand, making it clear in an instant that he cares absolutely nothing about the milk. But donuts? He crams a fluffy, fat hole into his mouth—then breaks into a smile.

"You like that?"

Oliver lunges for the bag, doing his best to grab it with glaze-crusted hands. "Ma ma."

He's probably wanting her to feed him. "Sorry, big guy. I'll have to do for now."

Suddenly, I hear a knock on the door and I tense. Who the fuck is that?

I consider not answering, but somehow this someone got past the security gate. Since I didn't hear anything screech or break, I'm assuming they have the code.

Hoisting Oliver off the counter, I creep to the front window. I see a swanky black SUV in the driveway with a crib mattress hanging out the back. This must be Trace's friends with a much-needed delivery.

Ignoring the little boy's whines as he tries to lunge out of my arms to reach the donuts, I open the door a crack to find a thirtyish man standing on the stone-paved porch. He looks big and fit with dark hair so perfect it's clear he spent a fortune on his super-precise cut. Expensive shades rest on top of his head. But it's his eyes that get my attention. They're the same striking green as Oliver's.

"Hi, I'm Griff." He sticks out his hand. "Trace said you need a crib?"

I'm confused, but I shake it. "Yeah. I'm Tanner. Come on in."

"Thanks." He steps over the threshold and shuts the door behind him. "Where's Amanda?"

"Sleeping. Last night was…"

"A lot, I'm sure." Then he directs his attention to Oliver, ruffling the boy's hair. "There's my little brother."

He didn't mean that literally…did he? "I'm sorry, what?"

"My little brother." While I'm numb with shock, he plucks Oliver from my grasp. The boy goes happily with a grin. "But I've gotta tell you it's weirder than hell to have a son older than my youngest sibling."

I'm so confused. "Wait. You and Oliver are both…Barclay Reed's children?"

"Yeah, you didn't know? There are a bunch of us here on the island."

So when Douglas Lund referenced his late friend's other offspring, he didn't just mean Cook. "Besides Evan?"

"Yeah. Maxon is my older brother. We grew up together, along with my younger sister, Harlow."

"Noah Weston's wife?"

"Yeah."

Come to think of it, she had the green eyes, too. "I had no idea."

"Bethany is my other sister."

"She used to be Barclay's right hand? That's what I heard anyway."

"Yeah, but I didn't meet her until last Christmas."

Mind blown. "Your dad had six kids by four different women?" As soon as the words are out, I realize he might think I'm being rude or judgmental. "Sorry. Just trying to understand who's related to who here."

He laughs. "It's confusing. But I think you're up to speed now, at least with what we know."

It's none of my business, but I'm curious. "You think there are more?"

"He fathered five of his six kids in a seven-year span—proudly. Then I'm supposed to believe he found the willpower or decency not to knock up any other woman for twenty-six years, before Oliver came along? Does that make sense to you?"

Given what he's said? "No."

"Me, either. So we're all looking for others. But I didn't come here to draw you our fucked-up family tree. Trace said you're bodyguarding Amanda, and Oliver needs a crib."

"Exactly."

"Where do you want to set it up?"

"Since Amanda is sleeping in the bedroom, you can leave the pieces here." I gesture to a corner. "I'll figure out how to assemble it later." Somehow.

Oliver chooses that moment to jerk out of Griff's grasp. He barely manages to get a hand on the boy again before he falls to the floor. And once his little feet hit the tile, he makes a mad dash back to the donuts.

Griff laughs. "Oliver clearly knows what he likes."

"And he's hungry."

"No doubt." Griff frowns. "You weren't going to give him milk out of a carton, were you?"

"Um…" I guess I'm not supposed to.

"It'll wind up everywhere except in his mouth. Where's his sippy cup?"

"No idea." Hell, I'm only half sure what that is.

Over the next hour, Griff kindly helps me dig up an appropriate cup in Oliver's diaper bag, sit him in a makeshift booster seat, then scramble him up a few eggs to go with all the sugar. As soon as the little boy is done demolishing his food, he seems content to sit with his thumb in his mouth and a toy truck in his hand.

And I dodged a bullet. If left to figure out how to take care of Oliver by myself, this morning would have been messy. "Thanks a lot. I'd offer you a beer…"

"It's fine. I gotta drive home. Britta is holding down the fort with our two boys. Jamie is almost four. Gray isn't quite three months old. Together, they're more than a handful."

"I'll bet." I've only got Oliver to contend with, and I'm already feeling out of my element. But Griff seems to have the Dad thing down. "So about that crib…"

Griff and I retrieve all the parts from his SUV, and he gives me a quick, dirty explanation of how to put it together before he grabs a bag with crib sheets and a few blankets, then sets everything together in a corner of the living room.

"Thanks." I shake his hand. "Really. I know Amanda will appreciate it, too. And I'd appreciate it even more if you could keep our location on the downlow."

"No sweat. Here's my number, in case you need anything else." He hands me a business card, then heads to the door. "I'll see you around."

Then it hits me. If he's Barclay's son and Amanda is Lund's daughter, maybe he knows more about her, especially what happened between her and his father.

"A question before you go?"

Griff turns back. "Sure. What can I do for you?"

"I need help with Amanda. She wants protection. Someone is after her, and the explanation I'm getting feels…off. An asshole with murder in mind would try to shoot her or maybe set her place on fire. But this guy? He came after her with a knife. That's a way more personal approach than a slighted client of Barclay's would suggest."

"I never thought about it, but since you have to get really close to someone to stab them, that makes sense."

"She doesn't want to tell me about her relationship with your dad…but I can't shake the feeling that I won't be able to figure out who wants her dead or why without more information. Can you tell me anything?"

"Besides the fact dear old Dad had a history of knocking up his assistants? No."

"So I've heard."

"And sharing them with his sons."

Did Griff just say what I thought he said? "You…"

"Partook of his assistant? Yeah. When I was in high school. Her name was AnnaBeth."

Holy shit. "Did Amanda know any of this before she went to work for him?"

"I don't know. Honestly, I never paid that much attention to her. She was my kid sister's age. So even when I'd spent summers home and hung out by the pool, Amanda was still jail bait. No matter how cute she might have been, I did my best not to notice." He presses his lips together. "But I think my dad did, even back then."

"Any chance he more than noticed?"

Griff takes a long time answering. "If I had to bet? Yeah. And I think she would have let him."

My gut seizes up. "Seriously?"

He shrugs. "I'm speculating; I have to say that up front."

But Griff seems smart, and I'd be stupid not to listen. "I still want to hear."

"After my freshman year of college, Amanda came out to Cali to spend a chunk of her summer with Harlow, like she'd done for years. And she still looked at my dad with puppy-dog eyes. But after a trip to Mexico with some friends following my sophomore year, I went home. Amanda was there. I didn't see curiosity in the way she stared at him anymore. I didn't see innocence, either. I saw heat. I saw hero worship. And I didn't like the lecherous way he looked at her in return. To be fair, it's possible she had sex with someone else and it emboldened her to—"

"No. At least I don't think so. She told her brother that your dad is the only man she's ever had sex with."

He winces. "Then my guess is something happened between them during that year."

But if Griff was in his first year or two of college... "How old would Amanda have been?"

"About fifteen."

Is he fucking kidding me? "Would your dad really have—"

"Oh, yeah. He liked females and he liked them young. Bonus if they were virgins. I knew how he thought."

I have a feeling there's a story there, but I can't get sidetracked. "Did your dad ever confide in you about whether he, um...deflowered Amanda?"

"No, we weren't close. And I don't have any proof he did it back then, but now that we're talking...my gut tells me yes."

It would explain a lot, like why an otherwise sensible girl let her life get so off track. If Barclay got his hands on her young and warped her thoughts while he defiled her, maybe he used their relationship to string her along and persuade her to give him everything he wanted...until he was ready to cut her loose. It would also explain why she's so disillusioned now by men and love.

"That son of a bitch."

Griff doesn't even try to defend the bastard. "That was my dad. Selfish to the core. If it made him happy, he didn't think twice about who he hurt in the process."

"If he only cared about himself, why did he share his assistant with you?"

The cynical twist of Griff's mouth is almost painful. "He wanted to create carbon copies of himself. If more of us were bent like him, then he couldn't be completely wrong."

"That's a fucked-up point of view."

"That was my dad."

Griff is bitter, and I don't blame him. "I feel sorry for you and your siblings. For his assistants. For everyone he hurt."

"There are a bunch of us. We've all done our best to pick up and move on."

"I feel especially sorry for your mom."

He scoffs. "Don't. She's a viper in her own right, and she helped Dad gather clients—no matter how she had to do it—so he could take their money." He sighs. "I lived with a lot of anger and distrust for years. That shit cost me an emotional fortune with Britta. Jamie was nearly three when I met him for the first time. If I hadn't turned my shit around, I would have spent my life chasing pussy and I would have ended up alone, just like him." Then he does his best to laugh. "Aren't you glad you asked?"

His speech was heavy, but he gave me a lot to think about. "I am, actually. Thanks for being honest."

"Brutally so, but… I've known Amanda most of her life. I'd like to see her stay alive long enough to be happy."

"I'm working on the alive part. Can you think of anyone who would want her dead?"

"No. But my mom's trial for being an accessory to embezzlement starts next month. Maybe there's something there?"

It sounds plausible. I'll dig into that if I need to. "Do you know a guy she'd be familiar with from home named Bruce?"

"Yeah. Did she mention him?" He seems confused.

"It's a long story."

Griff shrugs. "He's all right. A little stiff, but you know… When you grow up with a bunch of billionaires in private schools, you begin to believe your shit doesn't stink."

I wouldn't have any idea. "Think he could make Amanda happy?"

"I can't say. Honestly, I haven't seen the guy in, like, ten years. He may have changed. I have. Amanda has. So it's possible."

He's got a good point. "Thanks. If you think of anything else, let me know?"

"Sure. I don't know where Trace found you, but he's good people. If he hooked you up with Amanda, then he must believe you're a good guy."

"She's been through a lot."

"Amen. I'll check in with you later, maybe swing by with my boys so Oliver has someone to play with?"

"That would be great. Good to meet you, man."

"You, too."

He leaves with a wave, and I'm stuck looking at a dozen parts to the crib, a closed door to the woman I've sworn to protect, along with her son—and a fucking decision to make. Enough money to finally start over...or protect Amanda because she's beginning to mean something to me?

Chapter Five

For the next hour, I sit with Oliver in the living room. With one hand, I try to entertain him with the toys I find stashed in his diaper bag. With the other, I pull up the search engine on my phone and try to figure out what the fuck to do. It seems crazy to give up a much-needed fortune—more cash than I've ever had in my life—for a woman I met eight hours ago. And if I sold her out, I'd have to live with that.

But what if it's for her own good?

First things first, I hand Oliver a stuffed train—something new for him to chew on—as I look up Barclay Reed. He has his own Wikipedia page, which tells me he was someone important, notorious or not. There are pictures of him throughout his life. No denying he was a good-looking SOB, and the green eyes are unmistakable. Even into his fifties, he could have been mistaken for a guy a dozen years younger. There's sketchy information about his childhood and education, his marriage, as well as his kids, most of whom also have Wikipedia pages.

The article talks about his many affairs, lists Bethany, Evan, and Oliver as his illegitimate children, while echoing Griff's speculation that there are more.

The end of the article outlines his embezzlement scheme, the billions of dollars he stole, and his ultimate death at the hands of a former client here in Maui four months ago.

It's all good information, but nothing particularly helpful to keep Amanda safe. Clicking onto other search results brings me to message boards from amateur sleuths about how he perpetrated a crime of that magnitude and almost got away with it, attorneys-in-training discussing how they would prosecute or defend the case, and a forum for survivors of predatory bosses with a whole thread dedicated to Barclay Reed. Some of the stories from his former assistants and even women who interviewed for him make my stomach turn.

Then again, this is a man who was approaching fifty when he more than likely seduced a fifteen-year-old girl. It doesn't get much lower than that.

Other than feeling as if I need a shower after reading about this predator, I'm not learning anything new, so I start looking into Bruce. It takes me a while to figure out his last name, and I have to resort to the time-honored tradition of looking for Facebook friends of people in Amanda's life who might also be friends with him. A few minutes later? Bingo.

Bruce Barrett. And what do you know? He has a Wikipedia page, too. Age thirty-one. Co-founder of some hipster new investment firm. Heir of Wall Street royalty. Net worth over half a billion dollars, just like Lund Senior said. He's decent looking, a Yale grad, and a philanthropist according to what I'm reading. I glance through his bio. It's no shock he skated by in high school. There's speculation that his name and money paved his way to college. He was initiated into Skull and Bones, which means he knows all the movers and shakers who are fellow Bonesmen—senators, supreme court justices, heads of big investment banks, and even President Hayes.

There's a paragraph dedicated to high school antics and college pranks—everything from defacing a rival school's property to kidnapping their mascot, a hazing incident or two, and even a cheating scandal—but somehow he's always managed to come out unscathed. To me, that's not a mystery. That's just money.

I darken my phone and pry Oliver away from the double-glass doors leading to the beach. He wants out. He's a boy who wants to run and play, and I don't blame him, but I need more time to take stock out there and see if there's a safe area. Instead, I scoop him up and do my best to toss him in the air and mimic him flying over my head like he's an airplane.

I'm making zooming noises to the sound of his giggles when I hear the bedroom door tear open and Amanda lurches out, a long blond braid nestled between her soft breasts and a silken champagne-colored nightie barely covering the essentials.

My mouth goes dry.

Her panicked gaze lands on us, then she sighs with relief. "Oh, thank God. You've got Oliver, and he's okay."

"Of course. Did you think I wouldn't take care of him?"

"He's not your responsibility." She bustles closer, shoving her braid over her shoulder.

My mouth goes even dryer. I'd bet a hundred bucks she's not wearing a stitch under that nightie. Its spaghetti straps attach to a bodice that dips into a *V* that barely contain her breasts. Everything in front is covered...but when she plucks Oliver from my grip and turns to lift him against her, I realize the sides are made of nothing but transparent lace and the back is virtually non-existent. Everything between her neck and the curve of her ass is bare, except the two thin criss-crossing straps. Fuck, my mouth is so dry now I can't even swallow.

I hate to admit how hard my cock is.

"How long has he been awake?"

It's impossible to tear my stare away from her so I stop trying. "Um...a couple of hours. I gave him some breakfast. Then Griff came by with the crib, and..." I lose my train of thought when she turns her profile to me to cuddle her son—and I get a glimpse of the side of her pale, plump breast.

"Did you change him?" she asks.

"No." I should have and I didn't even think of it. "Sorry. It's my first rodeo with a kid."

"It's fine. Thank you for feeding him." She grabs the diaper bag, then disappears with Oliver into the master bedroom.

I find myself staring at a wall. What the hell am I going to do? I have to choose between restarting my future and safeguarding hers. And then there's all the awareness between us, complicating everything even more.

We need to talk. I need some answers. How does she feel about Bruce? What does she picture doing with the rest of her life?

Be honest. You want to know if you have any chance with this woman.

I hate that voice in my head, but it's right.

Fuck, we've talked about this. Amanda and I have no business getting tangled up in each other. She's a dozen years younger. I haven't even signed my divorce decree. I can't provide for this woman, especially in the way she's accustomed to. What the hell am I thinking?

That her family, even if they're well meaning, is controlling. They'll insist, even coerce her, into doing what's socially acceptable without caring what she wants or needs.

And if she was serious about wanting me, I wouldn't care about any of that. I would move heaven and earth to make her happy.

She emerges a minute later. Oliver is wearing a new pair of khaki shorts and a brown tank top with a monster truck on the front. She sets him on the floor in front of me with an iPad already streaming a cartoon. "Will you watch him for a minute while I get dressed?"

"Sure." I'm barely able to croak the word, just like I'm barely able to peel my stare from her silk-draped curves.

Amanda frowns. "Are you okay?"

"Yeah."

But I'm not. Am I seriously considering giving up the kind of money that could turn my entire life around for her? I should probably be asking myself if I've gone insane. I certainly didn't wake up this morning with any thought of getting involved again. Now I'm only thinking about Amanda and wondering if I'm the only one who's feeling something more than attraction.

"If you say so…" She turns away with a shake of her head.

"Before you go, I need to know one thing."

"What?"

I grab her wrist and tug her against me. Her breasts collide with my chest. I wrap my arm around her middle. Her gaze bounces up to mine, and I brace her nape in my palm. Her lips part. Then I can't resist dipping my head and taking her mouth with my own.

If I had any doubt our chemistry would be incendiary, I put that to rest the instant our lips meet. They're sweet and silky, pouty and yielding. They ignite an instant spark that burns through my blood.

I jerk her closer and nudge my way into her mouth, plunging inside to taste her. Amanda stiffens and gasps. Shit, she's going to slap me across the face and fire me. But no. She grabs my shoulders, presses her body against mine, and opens to me completely.

Oh, holy fuck. This woman is burning me alive—and I don't give a damn.

I fist her hair and press deeper into her mouth to drink in more of her sweetness. My hand suddenly takes on a life of its own, sliding from her waist, down the small of her back, to squeeze her pert ass and tuck her snugly against my aching cock.

I want her. Now. Sooner than now. I'm going to lose my damn mind before I get inside her. And it makes no sense. I've had my fair share of sex over the last couple of decades. I know how it usually feels and how I typically react to a woman. But this? I've never, ever felt this belly-lit, thought-crushing pleasure in my life. Until Amanda.

Is she with me?

I tear my lips away and stare down at her suddenly flushed face and slick, rosy lips. "Mandy? Say something, baby."

She's breathing hard, blinking at me, mouth agape. Finally she swallows. "What was that?"

"Something I couldn't stop. I'll apologize if you want me to, but I'll be lying."

"We already agreed getting involved would be a terrible idea." She steps back.

I'm suddenly transfixed at the sight of her nipples stabbing the front of her nightgown. Yeah, I got to her. "We did. But I'm starting to wonder if this attraction is stronger than us."

For a long minute, she says nothing. The only sounds I hear are Oliver's cartoon at our feet and her choppy breathing. She glances into my eyes, then her gaze drops to my lips. My heart lurches. Is she going to kiss me again?

"I'm not interested in just sex. I can't be."

"I'm not, either. Whatever's between us feels like more." Because I don't just want to take Amanda to bed, I want to see her protected and happy. Loved. And I can't see anyone else giving her that but me.

Yeah, I've lost my mind.

Instantly, she shakes her head. "No. I've been down this road, in a relationship with someone so wrong for me because the attraction felt too overpowering to resist. It doesn't lead anywhere good."

"That was Barclay. Don't compare me to him."

"That's not what I mean. I'm saying the pull between us—this hot, this strong, this quick—it's a lie. We have no future. I have a son to raise. You have a divorce to finalize. You don't know where you're living. I don't know where I'm living, either. I have no money, no job. And as far as I can tell, neither do you."

"We can figure that out together."

"Are you listening to yourself? How can you want me for anything beyond sex?" She tosses her hands in the air. "You've barely known me half a day."

Her father has underestimated Amanda. She's learned from her mistake with Barclay. She's trying to be logical and adult and make the most rational decision for herself and her son going forward.

And I'm dying for her to throw caution to the wind and let me do more than protect her.

"Maybe because I've been around the block enough to know that what we have is more than just attraction."

"I don't know if I can trust you—or any man—again."

"How do you know you can't? Are you going to spend the rest of your life alone? Are you going to deny what I can tell you're feeling"—I press a thumb over her pounding pulse—"because you're afraid?"

"It's not that simple. I have more than myself to think about."

She's right. And she's afraid that she'll let herself be carried away by her feelings again. So while taking her to bed might make us both feel damn good, that won't convince her to give us a chance.

"All right, then. Put on some clothes. I'll make you some food, and we can talk."

"If you have something to say, just say it."

I can't resist another visual skim of her curves before I force myself to look away. "If you keep wearing that silky, see-through thing and think I'll be able to have a productive conversation, you're insane. You look so gorgeous, and it's taking everything I have not to pluck you up and carry you off to the bedroom."

"Oh." She looks surprised. "I'll, um…be right back."

I nod, then lift Oliver, along with his iPad, carrying both into the kitchen, then set them on the tile. As I open the nearly barren refrigerator and absently check the expiration date on a container of strawberry Greek yogurt, I wonder what the fuck I can say to win Amanda's trust.

As I scramble another egg and toast one of the last pieces of bread, she returns to the kitchen, dressed in a springy turquoise sundress with spaghetti straps, a fitted waist, and a flirty hem that ends inches above her knees.

The dress does nothing to cool my libido.

"Is that for me?" She nods toward the stove.

"Yeah." Her toast pops up and her egg is finished, so I plate them, along with the yogurt. Then I set them in front of a nearby barstool before doing the same with utensils and a napkin. "Eat."

"I appreciate this. I'm starved," she admits as she sits.

"More coffee?"

She shakes her head. "Find any bottles of water?"

"A couple." I pluck one from the fridge and hand it her way.

"Thanks."

While she eats, we make small talk about the grocery order we need to place and the fact that Oliver will probably need another nap soon. We discuss the weather, then finally watch Oliver watching his cartoon in a silence so packed with awareness I swear the air is buzzing.

Finally, she's finished and stands. Together, we clean the kitchen, not exchanging a word.

I turn off the sink and say the only thing I think might convince her that I deserve her trust. "While you were sleeping, your father called and offered me a hundred thousand dollars to divulge our location."

"What?" She gapes.

"Oh, it gets better. There was an extra twenty-five thousand in it for me if I persuaded you to see Bruce Barrett and convinced you to marry him by Thursday."

Amanda shakes her head. "I'd be furious if it would do any good. He means well…"

"Maybe. But he doesn't understand you."

"What did you tell him?"

I could lie. Something pretty and not quite honest would prevent her from putting another brick in the wall between us. But if I want to win her trust, I can't. "That I'd call him back tomorrow and let him know."

"You didn't tell him to go to hell?" She laughs cynically and tosses her thick braid over her shoulder again. "I shouldn't even be surprised. You're not who I thought, and we don't have anything else to say."

When she tries to leave the kitchen, I block her path. "Really? I told you about his call, rather than disclosing our location and talking up this guy I've never met. That should tell you where my loyalties lie, baby."

"How do I know you're not confessing all this simply as leverage? If I agree to sleep with you, you won't tell my dad where to find me, but if I don't you'll be a hundred thousand dollars richer. It's a win-win for you."

"That's cynical. Barclay must have been a real"—I notice Oliver is suddenly watching us with big eyes—"jerk. I would never do that. I could have just seduced you."

"No, you couldn't."

"Wanna bet?"

She says nothing, just watches me with wary eyes.

"If I'd wanted to, I could have spent tonight inside you. Then tomorrow morning, I could have simply texted your dad our location, never mentioned his demand, then acted surprised when Bruce showed up to sweep you off your feet. After he took you away, I could have laughed all the way to the bank as I cashed my check. But I didn't. I'm being up front because I want your trust. Nothing between us will work unless you believe I'll take care of you. And unlike your dad, I'll do my best to respect your wishes, thoughts, and decisions."

Her expression softens. "Point taken. If you're so wonderful, why did you and...what's your wife's name?"

"Ex. All I have to do is sign the papers and pop them in the mail. Ellie is every bit as impatient to be done with our marriage as I am."

Amanda lifts a cynical brow. "How do I know that's true? You have no proof to show me, and Barclay told me some great stories. He was going to divorce Linda any day. She was being difficult, but he had great attorneys. The relationship falling apart was all her fault, of course. She only married him for money. She never loved him. And he never expected to find love with me, but he was going to move mountains so we could spend the rest of our lives together." She scoffs. "All lies."

That doesn't surprise me. "I'll never lie to you."

"Then why did you and Ellie split up?"

How the fuck do I explain this? "It's complicated."

"You cheated?"

"No."

"She cheated?"

"No. I could give you the canned answer that we grew apart. That's what I told my dad. But it's not one hundred percent accurate. The truth is, we both changed. And as I got older, I felt more compelled to help and shelter her from the worst of reality."

"She didn't like it?" Amanda sounds surprised by that.

"She hated it. Ellie's perspective has changed since we met. Now she sees my guidance as a sign that I think she's incapable of handling her own life. She also believes I wanted to take control because she's female. She's not completely wrong, but she's sure I did that because I thought she was inferior. That's not true at all." I shrug. "Over the last couple of years, I've figured out that I'm just wired to take care of the woman I'm with."

"Is that why you're attracted to me, because my brother thinks I need a 'daddy'?"

"Do you think you need one?"

"Answer me first." She sounds nervous.

"No. I was attracted to you before I even laid eyes on you. I heard you talking to Oliver from the hall at Nia's house, and just the sound of your voice did something to me. Setting eyes on you was an instant jolt."

"Me, too."

Good to know. "Now you answer me."

"I don't need someone to tell me what to do, and I resent my brother oversimplifying. I don't think he means to be sexist or dismissive. He just doesn't understand. What I want is a helpmate, a true lover in every sense of the word. Someone I can talk to, confide in. And…someone who will help protect me if there's a storm, so to speak."

Clearly, Barclay wasn't that man. "Exactly. And for the record, no. I don't think you need a 'daddy.' I think you need what I'm aching to give you."

"I'm not looking for someone to run my life or tell me what to do," she warns.

"I know, Mandy. You want someone who will be there *if* you need him." I brush my knuckles down her cheek, wanting to touch her so much more. "I can be that someone."

"I almost believe you. Are we crazy?"

"Maybe."

"You're not gun-shy from your divorce? It's not even final and—"

"It was final in every way but legally a long time ago. I've been ready to move on, and I've been searching. I think I stopped searching when I met you."

"I want to believe you…" But she's been burned—badly.

"I know. Wait here."

I push away from the kitchen counter and trek down the hall, into the little office beside the master. After stepping over the inflatable mattress, I rifle through my duffel until I pull out the thick envelope, then head back to the kitchen. "Got a pen?"

She rummages through the drawers until she finds one and hands it to me with a curious stare.

I open the envelope, unfold the thick pages of the divorce decree, then press the pen everywhere I see a tape flag, signing my name and ending my marriage for good. "Unlike Barclay, when I tell you the marriage is over, I don't mean that figuratively. I'm absolutely serious. These papers go in the mail tomorrow. Once the judge processes them, Ellie and I will officially be exes. Did Barclay Reed ever even try to divorce his wife?"

"No. He said he would, but…she ended up trying to divorce him."

"I'll never lie to you. I just want a chance to give you what you need."

"Why?"

"Because I think you can give me what I need in return."

Amanda reaches for me, then seems to think better and pulls her hand back. "I have to think about it."

"Sure."

She frowns. "What are you going to tell my father tomorrow?"

"To fu—" I see the iPad on the tile, forgotten, and Oliver still blinking up at us—"I mean, to pound sand."

"Really? Even without knowing if I'll choose you?"

"Yep. No matter what you decide." I cup her cheek. "I wouldn't blame you if you don't pick me. I'm broke and between businesses. I'm—"

"A seemingly good, honest man. And if you're everything I think you are, then I'd be a fool to turn you down."

"So don't."

She looks up at me. Her mysterious expression tells me her feelings run deep…but I can't read what they are. "Let me think. I'll let you know when I decide."

Chapter Six

As we finally finish the online grocery order and arrange a pick-up time, Oliver gets restless and cranky. We feed him the sliced turkey Masey left, along with some baby carrots. While Amanda cleans up after him and tries to soothe his fussy grunts and cries, I attack the crib Griff brought, glad I only need minimal tools, which he lent me, to assemble it.

Twenty minutes later, Amanda makes up the baby bed with clean sheets, then sets him in the master closet. "It's cooler and quieter in here, which helps him sleep."

She plugs in a nightlight just outside, in the adjoining bathroom, then leaves the master bedroom door cracked behind her. "We should be good for an hour or two."

"I think you're hidden here, at least temporarily. But have you given any thought to the idea that Oliver might be safer elsewhere?"

"There are a lot of pros and cons, no matter where he is."

"Sure, but let's be honest. No one is after him; they're after you."

She fidgets like she knows I'm right and hates to admit it. "Even so, I think keeping him with me is best for both of us."

I'm not his mom, so I can't argue her choice but… "Even though he's more of a target with you?"

"No one else will risk everything to keep him safe the way I will."

Maybe. Maybe not. Either way, she clearly doesn't expect her family or friends to put their lives on the line for her son. I'm still feeling my way around Amanda, but her choice isn't simply misguided insistence on being independent, despite the danger. I bet it has a lot more to do with her trust issues.

"While he's down, I'll start teaching you the self-defense I promised."

"I took some classes shortly after Barclay was arrested and I got accosted on the street for the first time. I could probably use a refresher later, but let's start with firearms."

I wish I'd been there to protect her. Losing her sense of anonymity and security must have been terrifying, especially when assholes started threatening her baby, too. "Sure. Let me go gather my gear, and I'll talk you through the basics."

"Where should we practice?"

"We won't be able to actually shoot here. Tomorrow, maybe some of your family can watch Oliver for a couple of hours so we can get to a gun range. It should be safe enough, and you'll need the practice. You'll need to be familiar with the weapon in your hand if you have to use it to defend yourself. You'll—"

"Can't we do it now?"

She's determined, and I appreciate that. Amanda never wants to be a victim again. "Let's try. I have an idea. I need to make a phone call."

"Thank you."

While she hustles away to find her purse and shoes, I pull out the card Griff gave me earlier—it tells me he's a Realtor—and give him a call. He and Britta are happy to help out, and their boys should both be awake in an hour.

When Amanda returns to the kitchen, I fill her in, then raid the last of Masey's leftovers in the refrigerator. As I put my plate in the dishwasher, Oliver stars howling from the other side of the house.

"He shouldn't already be awake. Ugh, his sleep schedule is so off," she groans as she jogs down the hall.

A minute later, she returns, carrying a plastic bag with a presumably wet diaper in one hand, while trying to balance the big hunk of boy against her chest with the other.

"I'll take him." I hurry to help her.

"Really? Thanks."

I ruffle Oliver's hair, and she smiles wistfully. "Barclay never held him, you know. Not once. For all the promises he made me and all the times he told me I was his world, when life got real his only priority was himself."

"If Reed wasn't already dead, I'd throttle him for the sheer joy of seeing the selfish bastard die." It's also too bad that the guy who offed Reed isn't still alive. I'd like to shake his hand.

Amanda blinks at me as if I've stunned her.

"Sorry, but I can't mourn a guy who took advantage of you, lied to you, then turned his back on you when it mattered most."

She shakes her head. "By then, I didn't mourn, either. Once Barclay walked away from me, I saw exactly the man he was—a terrible partner and father, not to mention a thief. If you had been first in line to kill him, I might have shoved you out of the way so I could do the honors. The world is better off without him."

Every time I think Amanda is soft and sweet, if a little mysterious, she completely blindsides me. She's tough when it counts. How else could she have fought off an intruder with a knife? How else has she endured months of a mob hunting her down?

I know I shouldn't touch her, but I can't resist. "I've never met a woman who's surprised me more. You intrigue the hell out of me, Mandy."

"No one has ever called me that. I kind of like it." She sends me another one of her Mona-Lisa smiles as she slips her purse onto her shoulder and we leave.

A few minutes later, we arrive at Griff and Britta's. The place is cottage-style and beachfront. The exterior looks charming. Then Britta opens the door to reveal a gorgeous interior, the back a solid wall of floor-to-ceiling glass doors that open to an expansive lanai overlooking the Pacific that would make most Mainlanders weep for their slice of paradise.

Inside, Griff is bouncing Jamie on his knee, while Britta, his pretty blond wife, invites us in, then follows behind, cuddling their infant.

"Forgive us. We only moved in a few months ago, and with the new baby, we haven't finished unpacking the last of the boxes."

Honestly, I hadn't even noticed. I was stuck on the sick ocean views.

"Angel, it's fine. Don't worry. They're here so Oliver can play with the boys, not to judge our organizational skills."

"I know, but I meant to be done by now, and I thought I'd have a chance to finish after Grayson was born, but…"

"One day at a time," Griff soothes her. "The morning sickness will go away eventually, then you can spend the last two trimesters 'nesting.'"

"You're pregnant again?" Amanda asks. "Congratulations!"

"Thanks. We found out earlier this week. We're going to tell the family tonight. It came sooner than we expected…" She sends Griff a scolding glance.

He sets Jamie aside with a ruffle of his hair, then saunters over to his wife and palms her belly. "I'm not sorry. I missed everything with Jamie. Seems like Gray arrived in a blink. Besides"—he kisses her forehead—"I love making babies with you."

She swats his arm, but she's trying to suppress a grin. "TMI. We have guests."

They have what I want. Funny how just this morning I was convinced that I'd put away all thoughts of marriage and babies and happily ever after. The truth isn't that I didn't want them anymore; I just didn't want them with Ellie.

I have a weird feeling things could be completely different with Amanda.

"I'm pretty sure they know where babies come from," Griff says in a stage whisper.

"You're incorrigible." She rolls her eyes, but I see her lurking smile before she turns back to us. "Can I get you two anything?"

"No, thanks," I say. "If we're going to get in some good practice rounds, we need to head out."

"We're here until six-thirty, so—"

"We'll be back way before then," Amanda promises, then hands Griff Oliver's diaper bag and jots down her number. "Call me if you need anything."

"You got it," Griff assures as he encourages Jamie—who's a big boy of not quite four—to play nicely with Oliver.

Then Amanda hugs her son before we hop back into the Mustang and head out to the nearest shooting range. "I'm going to rent you a collection of handguns to see what you like best."

"The smaller the better."

"Not necessarily," I tell her as I surge through a green light. "If someone breaks into your house with the intent to kill you, you need to put him down. Some small guns will only piss off an intruder. Smaller guns also have more kickback, meaning as soon as you pull the trigger they're harder to control, so the bullet won't necessarily go where you think it will."

"Oh, I didn't realize…"

"I'm going to start you with a couple of nine millimeter semiautomatics and thirty-eight revolvers. The latter is easier to use, but slower to load. It's a trade-off."

"What do you have?"

"A Glock. Great guns, but not optimal for someone with a child.

No safety. So we'll look at some others that make more sense for you and your use around home."

"All right."

We arrive a few minutes later, and I rent her a small collection of weapons, buy her some ear protection, grab a few paper targets, then carry everything into the indoor range. At our station, I show her how to load and unload each. I demonstrate how to make sure each gun is empty of ammo and how to store both the firearm and the bullets. Then I make her put everything into practice, loading the weapon and completing all the steps to ready it for fire. When I'm satisfied she's got the basics, I attach the target, then send it out into our lane with the press of a button. Not too far. She doesn't need to be a sharpshooter, and none of the guns I've selected are built for that. She just needs to practice putting someone down in a relatively close-combat situation, in case nothing else stands between her and death.

Finally, I show her how to hold the weapon and how to stand, adjusting her shoulders down and ensuring her fingers aren't anywhere near the trigger until she's ready to fire. But touching her inflames me. I'm all around her, feeling her softness, smelling that hint of flowers on her that drives me half-crazy, and watching her seriousness. She wants to learn, and I'm getting the clue that when Amanda focuses she can be relentless.

"Good. There's your target out there." I point. "Breathe normal and remember that, in real life, you'll be panicked. Your adrenaline will be rushing. It will be hard as fuck to focus. Remembering to breathe may be the one thing that steadies you in a crisis. It may mean the difference between life and death."

"Got it."

"Good. Now give your paper intruder hell."

She empties the first revolver and does fairly well. She doesn't hit the person drawn on the target more than once or twice, but if he'd truly been someone invading her place, she would have at least scared the piss out of him. Ditto with the second revolver, though she had more control over that weapon, probably because she's getting the hang of it.

"How are you feeling now?"

"Still a little jittery."

"Revved up?"

"Yeah."

"That's just a fraction of what you'll feel in a real-world situation."

She nods, then loads her first semiautomatic, slamming in the magazine like a pro. "I'll get this if I practice, right?"

"Absolutely."

"Good. Then next time someone breaks into my house, maybe I won't be so terrified because I won't have to come so damn close to the crazy man as I did when I hit him on the head with a vase."

"Let's go again."

I love the way she's determined. I'd rather be the one taking care of her, but if she won't let me, I'll feel a shit ton better knowing she's capable. And with her third weapon, she shows me she's getting more proficient.

"This is the last weapon for you to fire." I hand her the firearm and explain how it's different from the last nine millimeter she fired. "The trigger may be a little stiffer, but the barrel is longer, so you'll have less kickback."

She wraps her small fingers around it with a frown. "It's awfully big. And heavy."

"It's a double-stack, meaning there are two rows of bullets in the magazine, not just one. You may not need that for home security, but since they had this available as a rental, I wanted you to see the difference. Give it a whirl." I point out to the fresh target I pinned for her. "Try for head and chest shots."

I'd be happy if she hit the target anywhere on the body, but this will give her someplace specific to focus.

Amanda nods, then aims and fires. Instantly, I can see she's adopting all the adjustments I've given her since we started—and it's showing. By the time she empties the magazine, more than one shot has penetrated the paper intruder—one right between the eyes.

"You did fantastic," I praise.

"That felt surprisingly good. This gun was actually the easiest to use." She sets it on the counter, then smiles up at me.

She's pleased with herself, and she should be.

"I thought it might be, despite its size." I bring the target in and let her examine it, pointing out some of her best shots. "And you've never shot before?"

"Never."

"Honestly, if we keep practicing, I think you'll get proficient quickly."

Her lips curl up more, and I realize this is the first time I've seen her genuine smile. Not the one she pastes on to be polite. Not the one she gives me when she disagrees but doesn't want to say so. Not the one she flashes when she's keeping something secret. Not even the one she sends Oliver that shows how much she loves him. Best of all? This smile is only for me.

"I'm sorry," I tell her.

She frowns in confusion. "For what? Did I do something wrong?"

"When you look at me like that, I can't resist you." I palm her nape and seize her lips, falling into her pillowy softness and losing myself in everything that makes Amanda so lush and female.

She doesn't hesitate or pull back. Instead, she opens and gives me total dominion over her mouth. It's heady, and that does something to me because I know she doesn't trust easily. I pull her closer, deepen the kiss…and wish like hell we were someplace alone.

The guy in the lane next to us, who I'm pretty sure is an off-duty cop, starts firing. Mandy jolts. I pull back with a frustrated groan, which is drowned out by the sounds of more gunfire, and try to hide another erection. Fuck, I've been able to control my reactions for years. Around Amanda, I seem to have as much mastery over my body as I did at sixteen.

"We're done here. Let's go."

"Already?"

"We're out of ammo. Hopefully, we can come back soon." I load the rentals back in our borrowed case, take her hand, and turn the weapons back in. Then I lead her to the car. "So you liked it?"

"I'm surprised, but yes. It's a shockingly good stress reliever."

I laugh. Mandy is full of surprises—and I love that. She's on the small side and a girly kind of girl. I wasn't sure she'd be into shooting. Some women I've taught in the past were gung-ho to start, then found it too loud after a few rounds. Others still found the paper targets that resemble people too real and objected on principle. I get that, but when I'd push back and ask them if they'd registered for my class as a means of self or home defense—most had—they would say they didn't think they could pull the trigger if push came to shove. I disagree; the survival instinct is strong. But I always smiled and refunded their money, regardless.

"It is."

"You said earlier that you found a place you'd like to open a range?"

"I think so, yeah," I answer as I pull out of the parking lot.

"That's exciting. When are you going to do it?"

I shrug. "I need the money first."

"Is that why you agreed to bodyguard me this week?"

"No. Trace asked, and I always like to help friends. Then he mentioned they were threatening you and Oliver, and that just pissed me off. But I have to be honest. Everything changed when I saw you."

She gets quieter. "And?"

"I wanted you. It was instant. I worry about that, Mandy. A distracted bodyguard is a bad one."

"You've been great," she insists. "And I'm convinced you would protect me if someone threatened me."

"I would, but it seems like what you really want is to be able to take care of yourself."

"Do you blame me?"

After all she's been through? "No. I respect the hell out of it. And I want to help you."

"Even though you want to take care of the women around you?"

"Yes." But the truth is, I want to take care of Mandy more than I ever did Ellie. "I'm protective, not a pig."

That earns me another genuine smile. Then she shocks me by reaching for my hand and tangling her fingers with mine. "Show me where you'd like to open your range?"

"Sure." I hope her interest is a sign that she's starting to think about what something more than a week with me and as something more than her bodyguard would be like. "It's on our way to the grocery store."

I head down the highway, windows down, enjoying the warm Hawaiian air. In Colorado, we'd still be wondering if Mother Nature had another snow or two for us before spring bloomed. But Maui? It's eternal summer here. I'd never need another winter jacket or warm boots. I could live year-round in tank tops and flip-flops. That suddenly seems like paradise to me. It would be even better if I could persuade Mandy to stay with me and give us a try.

A few minutes later, I turn off the main drag and into a light industrial zone. It's not far off the beaten path, and there's a place to affix a sign to the building that would make it visible to the busy adjacent street. We drive around the block, and I describe what I'd do to the guest area, how I'd arrange the rentals, the gun sales, and the private lessons. Before I know it, I'm even telling her what I'd like to do with the firing lanes that differ from what we saw today.

When I finally glance at her as I ease back onto the highway, I'm grateful her eyes aren't glazed over. In fact, she has some ideas about how to make the whole thing more female friendly—and I welcome that. I want women to feel empowered and have the confidence of knowing they can protect themselves, their loved ones, and their children if they really had to.

"Thanks for the suggestions."

She shrugs. "Just my observations. They may seem silly, but I think they'd make a difference."

"If a few minor visual adjustments will help women relax and learn their best when they're with me, I'm all about it."

I get another genuine smile. "I love that your ego isn't the first thing you think about."

And I'll bet Barclay's was. "Nope. Everyone has a different perspective, and I'm always willing to listen. I may not agree, but I'm also perfectly comfortable respecting someone else's point of view, even if I don't share it."

"Me, too. Barclay…"

"Took it personally if you didn't fall in line?"

"He took everything personally."

"Why did you fall for him?" I can't resist asking. "I know it's none of my business, and you can tell me to shut the hell up, but you're so…"

"Naive?" she supplies, rolling her eyes at herself.

She was, but that's hardly her fault, especially if Griff's speculation is true. "I was going to say honest, caring, and reasonable."

Mandy sighs. "Thank you. But I think some of those traits were actually my downfall. I believed what he told me. I took it all at face value. I didn't question him as much as I should have because I wanted the illusion to be true so badly."

"I'm sorry he wasn't everything you thought he'd be."

"Not even close, but I learned a lot."

"Like what?"

She cocks her head. "Mostly? To trust my gut. I didn't listen to it at all with Barclay and I should have."

In some ways, I think I did the same with Ellie. At the very least, I didn't question the longevity of our connection. I definitely didn't second-guess where we were heading when we started growing apart. With Amanda, every instinct I have is telling me that we'd be good for each other, that I should hold her tightly and never let go.

"Did you love him?"

"For a long time, I thought I did. But I didn't know what love was."

Because when he first seduced her, she was too young to comprehend? "How did you two get together?"

The second the question is out of my mouth, her face closes up. "I'm not ready to talk about it. Sorry. Let's get the groceries, pick Oliver up, and make some dinner."

Subject closed. Because she's embarrassed; I sense that's at least part of it. The rest? Back to trust. The fact I don't have hers chafes, but we've literally known each other twelve hours. Hell, maybe I'm the crazy one for thinking thoughts of tomorrow, commitments, and our future. But acknowledging that isn't changing a damn thing.

"All right." I withdraw my hand and settle it back on the steering wheel.

"Tanner?" She moves her palm over to my thigh, surprising me.

"Yeah."

"I want to tell you, but I'm afraid you'll judge me."

It's a step forward. It's more honest than she had been even a few hours ago. "I won't."

"You don't know that," she argues. "I'm sure a lot of people would tell me I'm getting what I deserve. I knew what I was doing was wrong and I did it anyway."

"I'm not most people. I'm on your side. But I want you to feel comfortable. If you're not…you're not."

She's quiet such a long time, I'm sure the conversation is over. Finally, she sighs. "I'm still thinking. You know, about…us. But if we decide to try, um…moving forward, I'll tell you everything."

I wish she was giving me a different answer, but I can't make demands. "All right."

Short minutes later, we swing by the grocery store. After they settle the bags in the Mustang's backseat, we head to Griff and Britta's. The boys are all spread out on the living room floor. Jamie and Oliver are both rolling trucks around the carpet and making engine noises. Grayson looks on nearby as he props himself on his elbows and does his best to keep his wobbly head lifted. One thing I notice right away? He's got the Reed green eyes and his mother's blond hair.

Britta watches over the trio of tots with a smile. She's cleaned up since we saw them earlier, and she's now wearing a simple sundress with minimal makeup, along with a pair of springy, low-heeled sandals. "Hi. How was the shooting range?"

"Good." I turn to look at Amanda.

She nods enthusiastically. "I did better than I thought I would. For a first timer, I'll take that."

Griff lopes down the stairs a moment later, freshly showered and wearing a collared shirt with a pair of khaki shorts. "Hey."

"Hi, we'll take Mandy's little guy off your hands so you can get back to your evening."

"You're good. We're all meeting at Noah and Harlow's place for dinner in an hour or so, nothing fancy."

I pluck Oliver off the floor, and I'm not surprised when he spots his mother and lunges for her. Amanda takes him from my grip and holds him tight. "Missed you, little man."

"Ma ma."

"Was he good?" she asks.

"He didn't cry once. We fed him some juice and animal crackers, and he was fine," Britta assures, then plucks the baby from the floor and addresses her husband. "I'm going to feed Gray before we go."

"Sounds good."

"It was nice to see you." Britta smiles, then disappears upstairs.

"You, too. We'll get out of your hair," I say.

Mandy scoops up her son's diaper bag. "Thanks for everything, Griff."

"No problem. All the Reed siblings want a close relationship with Oliver, so I was glad to spend time with him. Anytime we're free, we'd love to—"

"Can I just say I'm sorry?" Amanda interrupts him.

He frowns. "For?"

"Not thinking about the harm I was inflicting on your family. Your father was married, and I knew it. I was too stupid to realize that, even if I thought my heart beat and bled for him, I wasn't the only person who mattered. I was so attuned to my own feelings that I forgot about everyone else. I can't tell you how much I regret that and how horrible I feel for tearing your family—"

"Don't. It wasn't your fault. We weren't really a family, and you didn't do any damage that my mom and dad hadn't already done to themselves." He frowns. "You know you're not the first woman Dad cheated with, right?"

She looks down. "I know. But at the time I wanted so badly for him to leave Linda."

"She would have deserved it because she was no saint, either. But he was never going to divorce her. He couldn't afford to. If anyone's sorry, it's me. I knew what kind of man he was when you went to work for him. I knew his history with assistants. I could have warned you and I didn't."

"I wouldn't have listened anyway. Some things you just have to find out for yourself." She peers at him uncertainly. "Would you think it's weird if I wanted to hug you?"

"Not at all." Griff gives her a brotherly embrace, and it's obvious she's relieved both to have the apology off her chest and that he's accepted it. "I always considered the Lunds family. I didn't know we'd ever be related by blood, but I grew up thinking of you like a sister, so I'm glad to welcome you into the fold. We'd love it if you stayed on the island."

"I'm actually thinking about it."

"You want to come to dinner tonight? I know Noah and Harlow wouldn't mind two more. Well, three." He grins as he brushes Oliver's rosy cheek with a big finger.

"I don't think it's a good idea."

"Why?" Griff pins her with a critical stare. "When was the last time you talked to Harlow?"

I jump in. I don't know if the reason for Mandy's refusal is the same as mine, but… "Whoever's out to get her is unhinged. I don't want to put anyone else in danger."

She latches on to my excuse with a nod. "Exactly. I wouldn't feel right if I hung out and put her in jeopardy."

Griff frowns like he understands but doesn't like it. "For you, she'd risk it. Do you need anything else?"

"Nothing, but thanks," she assures. "Tell Britta we said goodbye."

"Will do."

"Good luck tonight," Mandy calls as we leave.

Then we're gone. The ride back to the house is silent. She's so pensive, I can almost hear her thinking. I want to ask questions, help her sort through her thoughts if she needs it, and blurt all the reasons I hope she gives us a try. But I don't. Outside noise when I'm trying to think bugs the hell out of me, and I'm guessing she won't appreciate me "mansplaining," as Ellie would have put it.

Back at Masey's vacation rental, I hide the distinctive Mustang in the adjacent garage, then make a quick trip through the interior of the house. Nothing has been disrupted, so I lead Amanda and Oliver in. We settle the groceries, plan a quick dinner, then she disappears to give

Oliver a bath.

As I chop some veggies for a salad and heat the oven for chicken, I can't help but wonder what the night will bring.

When she emerges with a freshly bathed boy, she leaves him to play on a blanket with his toys, and we finish cooking. While she's picking at her plate, she's giving Oliver tiny bites of chicken and some jarred food we picked up at the store.

Finally, as the sun begins to go down, she disappears into the master bedroom with her baby. Then I hear singing. Her voice is high, light, and melodic. And I hear her love for Oliver as she croons the lullaby.

I can't help it. I meander down the hall and prop myself against the portal to watch. She's cradling her son against her chest, and he's looking up at her with big eyes. The naked love on her face as she looks down at him nearly chokes me. In that moment, I realize I'd consider myself incredibly blessed to have even a fraction of the devotion she's showing her son. And I find myself determined to win her. I want more days like today. More nights where she sings Oliver— and maybe the children we have together—to sleep. I don't care if it sounds crazy anymore. I'm listening to my gut.

Suddenly, she looks up and catches sight of me. "What are you doing?"

Her whisper isn't meant to be sexy, but somehow it lights me on fire. "Watching you. You're beautiful. Barclay was an idiot for throwing you away."

Her lips curl up in a shy smile. "You're only saying that because you're trying to seduce me."

"No. Well, yes, I'm trying to seduce you, but I'm saying that because it's true." I lean against the doorway. "Is it working?"

Chapter Seven

After Oliver fell asleep, cuddled up with his plushy toy train, Mandy and I do the dishes in silence. I can tell she's thinking—so hard I can almost feel it.

She's in the middle of drying a frying pan when she abruptly turns to me. "How long were you married?"

"Ten years officially, but Ellie and I have been separated for nearly two. She asked for 'space' one night. A few months later, I realized I was more relaxed, more…myself—not walking on eggshells, wondering if I was saying the wrong thing all the time—so I filed for divorce. She didn't fight me."

"No children?"

I shake my head. "We tried. Eventually doctors told us she wouldn't be able to get pregnant." No reason to get into all the medical stuff, and I doubt Mandy cares about my ex-wife's ovaries. "It's one of the things that changed her perspective on life, I think. After we heard that without something like IVF she wouldn't be able to have kids, she started focusing on ways to improve herself, which I supported. She wanted to go to college. Fine. I was busy with the gun range. She helped when she could. But…we started living two different lives and grew apart."

"Did you want children?"

"Yeah."

"Do you still?"

I tucked that hope away years ago, after the doctors gave Ellie and me the bad news and she refused to discuss adoption. But now? "If the opportunity arises, I'd like to. The sooner the better. I want to be young enough to enjoy them."

Mandy nods. "Is Ellie your age?"

"Six years younger."

"Do you think the age difference was the problem with you two?"

The easy answer is no. When Ellie and I got married, we were both in our twenties and at roughly the same place in life. But I'm not sure that's what Mandy is really asking. "Maybe. I don't know whether the age difference had anything to do with her refusal to try working it out. Maybe it was immaturity. Or maybe it was the realization that her thirties were just starting and she didn't want to spend them tied down to someone she didn't see a future with?" I shrug. "I don't know. But she was always looking for something. Herself, I think. I'm not sure how much of a role age played in that."

"Thank you. I'm not trying to be invasive." She sets the frying pan aside and blinks up at me in the too-bright kitchen. "I'm trying to figure out if we'd be a good fit."

I suspected as much. "Take your time. When you decide, I want you to be sure."

"Does my age bother you?"

"I've given it thought, but no. Does my age bother you?"

She shakes her head. "I was never attracted to anyone my own age. Even in fifth grade, I had a crush on my teacher."

"When did you first think of Barclay as something other than your dad's friend?"

"Honestly? I don't think I ever saw him that way." Mandy hesitates. "It's funny. My mother was always reluctant to let me spend summers with Harlow at the Reed house because she worried Maxon or Griff would try to hustle me into bed."

"Did they?"

"Never."

"Were you ever interested?"

She wrinkles her nose. "They were like older brothers to me, teasing, tormenting... So no."

I nod, taking that in as I put away the last of the dishes while she wipes down the counter. "Be right back."

"Sure."

A few steps later, I exit the front door into the Hawaiian night. The breeze is balmy, the air perfumed. I flip on my phone's flashlight and check the front gate. No evidence of tampering, and it's shut tight.

Then I walk the perimeter of the house. Since there's no fence at all in back—wouldn't want to block the ocean view—there's nothing to deter intruders. I wish the house itself had an alarm system. That wouldn't be fool-proof, either. But an extra layer of security would give me some peace of mind. The best I can do now is to hope that Mandy's would-be killer has no idea where to find her—and be ready in case he does.

After ensuring both the front and back doors are locked tight, and checking the windows for the second time today, I'm satisfied that Mandy and Oliver are as safe here as they can be.

When I enter the kitchen again, she's finishing a conversation. "Call me tomorrow and let me know you're okay. Yes, I'm fine." She pauses. "Oliver went right to sleep. He was exhausted. When will Evan be home?" Another pause. "Good. Stay with Noah and Harlow until then. Sounds like they could use the extra pair of hands since Noah's mother hurt her ankle." A last pause. "You, too. Good night."

That must have been Nia. "How's your sister?"

"She's all right. She took your advice and decided to stay with family until her husband returns from London on Wednesday."

I approach Mandy, fighting one hell of an urge to put my hands all over her. Instead, I cup her face. "You look tired, baby. Why don't you let me tuck you in?" When she raises a brow at me, I shake my head. "Just sleep."

"It's too early. If I go to bed now, I'll be awake at three a.m. But I'm too tired to return most of these texts and calls I missed earlier."

"From who?"

"Well, I did text my brother back. Otherwise, he would have sent out the National Guard, but Maxon will have to wait until morning." She sighs. "And Bruce."

That raises my hackles. I have no reason or right to be jealous...but I can't help it. "What does he want?"

"All the predictable stuff. He wants to know where I am so he can come out here and talk to me. He's crazy enough to do it, too."

That sends off alarm bells. "Is he crazy enough to harass and threaten you?"

She frowns. "I can't even picture that. Bruce doesn't seem like the violent kind."

Maybe not, but anyone with enough motive can become violent.

"Besides, why would he try to hurt me when he says he just wants me to know how deep his feelings for me are?" She falls quieter. "He wants me to marry him."

I stiffen. "How do you feel?"

"I've resisted because I've worried he has his nose too far up my father's ass. But since Dad tried to buy you off so Bruce could marry me, I'm convinced. Nice to know my instincts were right."

"Sounds like." I'm just glad she has no interest in Bruce. If I make Mandy mine, he's one less bastard for me to fight off.

"Now that Oliver is down, I'm going to take my evening shower. I'll be back."

While she does, I find the pump to blow up my inflatable mattress, fit it with some sheets stashed in the closet, grab a quilt and a pillow, and hope it will be comfortable enough to catch some z's.

When I'm done, I saunter out to the living room to wait. A moment later she emerges, looking clean and wearing a short, silken champagne-colored bathrobe belted around her small waist. A thick braid falls over one dainty shoulder. Her feet are bare.

I'm instantly turned on.

What would it be like to go to bed with her every night and know she's mine?

"Oh, I feel so much better. Best part of the day, after a long shower and once I'm wearing my favorite frilly nightie." She stretches, and I try not to look at her rising breasts or her short hem making its way up her thighs. "TV?"

"Sure." I don't watch much, but if it makes her happy—and takes my mind off sex—fine.

We both plop onto the sofa, then turn to each other with a matched set of scowls. She's gaping in shock. "This is the hardest sofa I've ever sat on. There's nothing comfortable about it."

I nod. "It's like a damn rock."

We end up on the floor together since the rug is actually softer. I lean back against the hard-as-stone sofa. Mandy falls against me and curls up to my side, and it seems so natural when I wrap my arm around her. She rests her head on my shoulder as I flip on the TV.

"What do you like to watch?"

"Anymore? I barely have time. But I don't want to get too involved, so no bingeing."

"Sure." I flip a little and find the start of a house hunting show. "This work for you?"

"I love these shows. You ever watch them?"

I didn't even know these were a thing. "Can't say I do."

Over the next thirty minutes, we see a same-sex couple trying to choose a new house in Phoenix. At the end, we both agree house two is the better option, even though it's a bit of a fixer. But the couple on the show picks house one because it's move-in ready.

"I don't get that." She gestures to the TV. "A little elbow grease can be fun, and you get to make the place your own."

I shrug. "Yep. Besides, the house they picked seems way too small."

"Totally."

Another episode starts, this time starring a single woman buying her first place after a divorce. She wants to be in the heart of Chicago, close to all the restaurants, bars, and her friends. Option number one is astronomically expensive, and when I look down to say something to Mandy about it, her eyes are closed. Her breathing is deep.

She's fast asleep.

I smile at her, then lift her into my arms, haul her against my chest, and head for the master bedroom. She doesn't weigh much, and it seems even more mind-blowing that she fought off a knife-wielding intruder alone.

Inside the cool, dark space, I tip her onto her feet and steady her. "Time for bed, Mandy."

"Wha...?" she mumbles, barely opening her eyes.

I'm not shocked she's exhausted. Sure, she napped earlier, but not nearly enough to make up for the six hours of sleep she missed last night.

Banding one arm around her waist, I pull the covers back, then peel off her silky-soft robe. Underneath, she's wearing that champagne nightie I saw earlier that reveals at least as much as it covers. Forcing myself not to gawk, I lay her down, head on the pillow, then cover her.

"Good night, Mandy." I kiss her forehead.

She doesn't even stir.

Smiling, I back away, then follow the faint golden glow of the nightlight into the walk-in closet. Oliver is sprawled on his back in the middle of the crib, his stuffed toy train cuddled in one lax palm.

He really is a cute kid. If Mandy decides to give us a chance, I'll be spending a lot more time with him. Even twelve hours ago that would have terrified me because what do I know about kids? But now I don't mind. In fact, I kind of like it.

On my way back out of the master bedroom, I glance at Mandy one last time. She's already grabbed the spare pillow and rolled to her side. I draw the black-out drapes, hoping the darkness will keep her asleep come sunrise. Then I double-check both the interior and exterior of the house, tightening locks as I go, before retreating to my makeshift bedroom to scan my phone. It's still early. I'm not quite tired, and nothing on the device is holding my attention.

What about Mandy's phone?

I shouldn't snoop or pry, but I need to make sure her location services are turned off. I don't know if her father or anyone else can ping her device and view her whereabouts. I fucking should have thought of that earlier, but the last time I did any bodyguarding work, tracking phones wasn't a thing.

With a sigh, I manage to work my way upright from the floor and find her device in the kitchen. It's not password protected, which is a bonus for me now...but I'll need to persuade her to correct that later. A quick scroll proves she doesn't have much on the phone except pictures of Oliver. Her emails are scant and mostly informational— news headlines, bills, bulletins from her alma matter, and the like. True to her word, she has no social media loaded. In her settings, I see her location services are turned on. Cursing, I press the button to shut them off. But if her father or anyone who's had access to her phone has already seen her current whereabouts, she's compromised.

If that's the case, I'll need a quick Plan B.

When I'm back at the home screen, I settle my thumb over the button to darken her phone when a text appears. It's from Bruce.

Please tell me where to find you. I'm worried.

"Motherfucker." I wish this guy would go away.

But he won't, and neither will her father—unless and until she tells them to.

I shouldn't do it. I know I shouldn't, but I start reading their text string, which started a few hours ago. And I get pissed.

I just heard from your dad that someone attacked you last night. Are you okay?

Fine. Thanks.

Let me protect you. Tell me where you're staying. I need to see you, to talk to you about us. You shouldn't have to protect Oliver alone. I'll be there for you.

We're friends, Bruce. I'm not ready to talk about more. I've hired a bodyguard, so I'm safe. Don't worry. We'll talk when I'm home.

I'm not giving up on you.

Mandy didn't reply after that, and this asswipe is texting her again. Doesn't he know when to quit?

She may not be cynical enough to question whether this jackhole is being paid to care so damn much, but I am. Sure, I understand why a father may want to make sure that his daughter finds a good husband. But Douglas Lund is going about this like a controlling bastard who didn't like Mandy's previous decisions so he's decided to make her future ones for her.

It's not going to happen, pal.

I darken her phone, traipse back down the hall, and after a pause to ensure she's still sleeping peacefully, I grab some clean boxers and find the bathroom on the other end of the villa. After a short, scalding shower, I arrange my Glock beside the mattress, within easy reach, then fall onto the inflatable again, lace my fingers across my stomach, and stare at the ceiling, wide awake. I'm hyperaware of Mandy in the next room.

It's going to be a long night.

Somewhere after midnight, I finally drift off and have a few weird-ass dreams I barely remember. I don't know why I'm suddenly awake. Then I hear footsteps in the hallway just outside the room. I tense and reach for the weapon, pointing it at the doorway just in time to see a shape emerge from the shadows toward me.

"Tanner?"

"Mandy," I breathe and shove the gun aside. "Something wrong?"

"I can't sleep."

Despite her exhaustion? I get to my feet and grope unsuccessfully for my T-shirt and shorts. "You afraid, baby? Don't be. You're safe. I'm making sure of it."

She fumbles through the dark until she grabs my hand. "I…I need you."

Given how independent she's had to be since Oliver's birth and how difficult it is for her to trust, admitting that couldn't have been easy.

"Sure."

"Thanks." She tugs on my hand and leads me toward her bedroom.

"Let me grab my clothes."

"No. Now. Please."

There's a note of need in her voice that pulls at me. I grab my Glock. "Would you feel better if I checked all the doors and windows again? Went through the house, top to bottom, to make sure we're alone?"

"I'm not afraid of an intruder right now." She reaches the side of the bed and flips on the nearby lamp. She's looking right at me. "I'm afraid of how I feel."

Tears sheen her eyes, and I can't resist setting my weapon down and cupping her cheek. "Why?"

"I swore I'd never fall for anyone again, and in one day you're about to make a liar out of me. I feel so close to falling…"

Is she serious? My heart revs. I take her other cheek in my palm until I'm cradling her face and staring into her eyes. "You don't have to be afraid. Go ahead and fall as hard as you want. I'll catch you."

"It's not that simple." She presses her lips together like she's fighting not to let those tears roll down her cheeks. "You don't know…"

"Then tell me."

Mandy looks torn. "You may not look at me the same after you know the whole truth."

Is she talking about Barclay? Is she going to divulge the details about their affair? Has she decided to give us a chance? "Yes, I will."

"Maybe you shouldn't."

The self-defeat in her tone hurts. "You can tell me anything, baby. As long as we're communicating, it's going to be fine. What do you need to talk about?"

"We shouldn't go any farther until you know what happened with Barclay. And if you can't forgive me, I'll understand."

I can't imagine why she thinks the story will make a damn bit of difference to me. But the look on her face says she's terrified it will.

"I just appreciate the truth." I guide her to sit on the mattress, then sink down beside her. "Go ahead."

She wrings her hands and takes a deep breath. "I always had a thing for Barclay Reed. I think I was…ten, maybe, when I first thought about him romantically. That sounds silly, but I mean in a first-crush, teen-heartthrob kind of way. I had pictures of him. I envisioned what it would be like for him to look at me like *that*. I imagined him kissing me. But I had no expectations until I turned thirteen."

"Thirteen?" My eyes bulge.

"Oh, nothing happened then," she assures me. "Except…he

looked at me. Just once. But that's all it took for me to be convinced I was in love and we were fated to be together."

I want to kill the bastard all over again for ogling a child. "Exactly how did he look at you?"

"Like a woman. That summer I was spending a few weeks with Harlow, as I usually did. The Saturday before I flew home, she and I were hanging by the pool. He sauntered into the backyard and said something; I don't even remember what. I just remember standing on the deck, getting ready to dive in again, when he pinned me with this gaze. I shivered, despite how hot the day was. The bottom of my feet were burning, but I was frozen by his stare. My cheeks got hot. My stomach fluttered. He scanned me from head to toe. I knew exactly what he was thinking."

"You were a girl."

She nodded. "But I didn't feel like one. And I didn't want him to see me as one."

"Then what?"

"Nothing that summer or the one afterward. The summer before I turned sixteen…that's when everything changed."

Just like Griff suggested. I feel myself get even tenser. "Did he seduce you then?"

"Yes…and no. We had sex." She licks her lips. "But I was the one who initiated it."

Is she kidding?

She jerks her stare down to her hands. "You look horrified. I don't blame you. When I say it now, I am, too. But you have to understand. I'd been completely obsessed with him for fully a third of my very short life. I couldn't imagine ever feeling differently about him. Back then, I was convinced I loved him and that he would love me too if he just knew how I felt. It was dumb and naive—"

"It doesn't matter. He took advantage of you. You were a child, and he was a grown-ass man who should have said no."

"That's what my therapist always says. And you're both right. As an adult I see that, but that night I saw an opportunity to be with him and I took it."

So did he. I grind my teeth together. "What happened?"

"Stephen, Dad, and I were supposed to go camping for the week with Barclay, Harlow, and Griff. We'd done it the summer before and had a great time. But Griff never showed. He and a bunch of college buddies ended up in Mexico instead. Harlow got sick the night before we left, throwing up everywhere. My dad suggested cancelling everything, but Barclay insisted we still go. When Harlow got better, Linda could drive her up to the site, no problem. So the rest of us went. Everything was fine the first day, but as night fell, Stephen started throwing up, and we thought he'd caught what Harlow had. Then he started running a fever, too, and complaining about excruciating abdominal pain. My dad panicked and drove Stephen to the nearest hospital—and just in time. He had an emergency appendectomy an hour later."

"That left you and Barclay alone."

She nods, a heart-rending mixture of guilt and shame wrenches her soft face. "It was too dark to pack up the campsite and head down the winding mountain road, so Barclay told my dad we'd leave at first light. I was so thrilled. Worried about my brother, yes. But I was determined to make the most of my time with Barclay. We had dinner, but we didn't talk. We eye-fucked."

I'm furious. Mandy was just a kid. Yeah, maybe she'd been developing a woman's body, but she had visions of Barclay being a romantic hero. The asshole should have been a responsible adult, not a predatory lech grooming her to be his underage sex partner.

"Amanda…" I don't know what she's planning to say next, but I want it to stop. "You don't have to tell me anymore."

"I do. Everyone blames Barclay for what happened. But I had a hand in it. I can't deny that."

"You didn't know any better."

"I didn't stop to think about the future or the consequences or anything like that, true. But I was pretty sure I knew what would happen when I lunged at him and pressed my lips to his."

I want to block this out, but she seems compelled to tell me. I can only guess it's because she's trying to gauge whether we have a future. And she won't trust any assurance I give her until she's spilled all the gory details.

"He kissed you back?"

She nods. "From the second our lips met, it was on. We climbed into the tent, and my clothes were off two minutes later. I helped him get me naked."

There's the self-blame in her voice again, and I'm so angry that I'm struggling to keep my temper in check. "Look, I know where you're going with this. If you think he only had sex with you because you encouraged it, you're wrong. From what I've heard of this guy, it was just a matter of time before he hit on you. Stop blaming yourself. He's the one who took advantage of your eagerness and naiveté."

"I wasn't so naive that I didn't know we were going to have sex. In fact, that's what I wanted." She frowns. "I just didn't expect it to be so rushed and to hurt so much."

That pisses me off even more. I don't want details but… "Did he just jump on you and shove his way inside you?"

She flushes and looks down. "More or less. And I did everything he told me to since I figured he knew what he was doing, but it wasn't as if we'd planned anything. Except…" She frowns. "He had condoms. So…yeah."

"He was prepared, then. Why else would he have brought them on a camping trip with his buddy and their kids unless he had a plan?" Granted, he couldn't have plotted Stephen's appendicitis, but he may have been cooking up something else in the hopes of getting Amanda alone. "It wasn't your fault, Mandy. Even if you thought you wanted to have sex with him that night, you were too young to understand everything that would follow."

"I think you and my therapist speak the same language." She tries to joke. "But you're right. I never stopped to think about the after part. I convinced myself that life would be perfect if he wanted me, too. And, of course, I was sure he would never have sex with me if he didn't love me. I'd known him most of my life, so it never occurred to me that he would hurt or use me."

At fifteen, she had no way of knowing how crazy lust and the forbidden drive some men. "So you were surprised when your life wasn't perfect after he took your innocence?"

"Yeah."

"He didn't love you, Mandy."

"He didn't."

"He preyed on you."

"I know."

"And he hurt you."

"A lot. I mean, I expected losing my virginity to be painful. A couple of my friends had already done it with their boyfriends, so they told me. I even overheard one of Stephen's girlfriends talking to him about her disastrous first time with another guy. But I expected Barclay to care, you know. But he was so impatient. It was horrible." She shakes her head. "And I was such an idiot. I wrote off his rush as passion neither of us could control."

I don't blame her for trying to make the unnecessary pain he'd inflicted fit with the world view she saw through her rose-colored glasses, but she simply hadn't been worldly enough to know that Barclay could have done so much to make the experience good for her.

"Did he apologize afterward?"

She laughs bitterly. "No. He kissed me again, told me he'd been wanting to do that for two years, and was glad I was willing to let him. Then he swore the painful part was over, donned another condom, and…we did it again."

"Jesus." Barclay Reed was clearly not just a pig and a pedophile, but a selfish asshole, too. The world is better off without him. I wonder how Griff turned out to be a seemingly good guy with half his genes and an upbringing courtesy of Barclay. It's a miracle.

But the look on Mandy's face tells me she's expecting my condemnation. "I've shocked you."

"You didn't, baby. He did. He should have known better. He should never have touched you." I rake a hand through my hair. If this is hard to hear, I'm sure it's doubly hard for Mandy to tell me. "What happened next?"

"I learned one thing about Barclay fast; he was insatiable. I don't know where he got the stamina, but we spent most of the night having sex."

"You must have been sore and exhausted and…" I'm stunned, and frankly, a little sick to my stomach.

"Completely. I told him that, too."

"And he still wouldn't leave you alone?"

"No, but I didn't ask him to. I wanted to be everything he needed. I was still convinced he would only be with me if he loved me, especially after he introduced me to the wonderful world of orgasms." She gives me an acidic, self-deprecating twist of her lips. "Barclay was a lot of things—a liar, a thief, an asshole. But once my hymen was no longer in the way, he was incredible in bed. I'm ashamed to admit that, for a long time, I took pleasure as a sign of love."

"I'm sure that was far more about his ego."

"Completely. I know that now." She looks away. "Long story short, Stephen was fine by the time we got to the hospital. I lied to my father about why I looked so tired and was walking funny. Barclay backed up my story, all while winking at me behind Dad's back like he loved the secret we shared. A few days later, as he hugged me goodbye at the curb at LAX, he whispered that my pussy was his and I'd better not share it with anyone. I promised I wouldn't. And for the next seven years, we carried on in secret. We grabbed every opportunity to be together we could. I even chose a college in Southern California to be closer to him. He lived in Maui at the time, but there weren't any acceptable universities on the island. He was often in LA for business, though. We usually spent a few nights a month together."

"And you still thought you were in love with him?"

"Absolutely. But when my senior year started, I really began thinking about our future. We spent a weekend together during my fall break, and I broached the topic of him leaving Linda." She shakes her head at herself. "I was having my doubts that Barclay loved me. I tried to assure myself he must, but I still wanted him to prove it in some way."

"What was his reaction?"

"He said he wanted to divorce Linda, but he had to move money around or she would bankrupt him. He said it would take a while. I understood him not wanting to give her half of his life's work. Remember, I'd known Linda most of my life, too. She'd always been cold and unlikeable—at least to me. So I convinced myself their problems were of her making, probably so I wouldn't have to see Barclay's faults...or my own." She shrugs. "Anyway, his answer disappointed me, but I was young. I had time. So I resolved to be patient. Then he moved from Maui back to LA and suggested I come to work for him after graduation so we could spend more time together while he got everything in order. I thought those were signs that he wanted to be with me."

More so he could keep fucking her under everyone's nose. "When did you figure out you two had no future?"

She's quiet a long time. "At first, it was little things. The day I started at Reed Financial, this guy who reported to him—a total jerk named Byron—called me the 'fresh meat.' He said he wasn't surprised that Barclay had hired me to replace his last assistant, who had just turned twenty-eight, since she was way past her prime."

"He sounds like an absolute jackass."

"A hundred percent. Then he said there was an office pool among his managers as to how long it would take Barclay to nail me. I was flabbergasted, but when I asked Barclay about it later, he told me Byron was an ass looking to stir the pot and that I should ignore him. Then I started hearing rumors about Barclay's flings with past assistants, along with the fact that he'd also talked to them about wanting to leave Linda, but never did. During all this, Barclay and I would sneak away for quickies in cars, conference rooms, and airplanes. Occasionally, we'd find ourselves a hotel suite. But I began to feel like a convenience, not a girlfriend. Not the woman he wanted to spend his life with. Eventually, it hit me that we never had sex in either of our respective beds. My first few months out of college, I shared an apartment with Harlow to manage expenses, so Barclay never wanted to spend the night there. Of course, he never invited me to his house with Linda unless my whole family was in town. But it occurred to me that if we were going to have a future, shouldn't we start telling the people in our lives about us? He just kept brushing me off, saying it wasn't the right time. And before you comment, yes, I should have known by then he had no intention of marrying me, but I didn't know how to stop hoping. I believed with all my heart that I loved him."

"What ended it?"

"I got pregnant. He claimed he'd had a vasectomy…so I went off the pill. What was the point of taking it if I didn't need to actually prevent pregnancy? My periods had always been regular…but I missed my first one after that. At first I told myself that my body was taking a while to restart normally, but when I vaulted out of bed one morning because I had to throw up, I knew."

"And you told him?"

"Immediately. In a way, I was relieved. I'd been stunned when he told me he'd gotten fixed. How were we going to have kids in the future if he'd had a vasectomy? Yes, he had children with Linda, but I was going to be his new wife and I wanted kids." She scoffs at herself. "When I told him I was pregnant, his first reaction was to grin, so I thought he was happy. Then he literally patted himself on the back and said he still 'had it.'"

Just when I'm convinced Reed couldn't be any worse, she proves me wrong. "What an asshole."

"And I really didn't figure that out until I asked him what we were going to do about Linda, his divorce, our future… He looked at me as if I was an idiot and told me he wasn't planning on doing a damn thing. He would leave Linda on his timetable, not mine. Then he said he'd been trying to figure out when I'd catch on to the fact that I was just a convenient hole. He'd enjoyed getting me pregnant, but he had enjoyed knocking up more than one of his assistants in the past, too. He, Byron, and some of the other managers even had a betting pool on me, and he won because he'd managed the feat so quickly. But he didn't want me anymore, especially since he hated fucking pregnant women. And he'd never loved me anyway. It probably sounds stupid, but I was shocked."

"Not stupid. Horrifying. Calling him an asshole is too nice."

"You're right. But I was still gaping and reeling when he told me I should consider our time together a life lesson, that I should think more critically and be far less gullible before I climbed between the sheets with someone else. And, by the way, I was fired. If I went quietly, he would give me six months' severance and pay me for the rest of my unused vacation time. If I thought about doing something silly like hiring a lawyer, going public, or telling my dad who'd fathered my baby…well, he already had an insurance policy. About a month prior, he'd asked me to grab the office's petty cash fund and stash it at home because, according to him, someone had been stealing from him. I did what he asked, and he made sure the office surveillance captured me 'stealing' so the police and the public would know I was accusing him of inappropriate behavior in the office to sling mud and cover my tracks." She folds her hands together. "Apparently, he'd run this same scam on several of his other assistants. It always worked."

I can't even understand Reed's depravity and I don't want to waste time trying. Instead, I take her hand in mine, doing my best not to betray the depth of my anger. "I don't even have a word low or filthy enough to call that man. Really, if he wasn't already dead, I'd be hard pressed not to hunt him down and pull the trigger myself."

"Thank you for taking my side, but it's hard not to feel like the blame is half mine. I wanted so badly for the shimmering future I could picture with him to be real that I gave myself easily, made excuses, and overlooked obvious red flags." She sighs. "So trust is hard for me now. I especially have a hard time trusting myself."

And that's the biggest problem. She wants to believe we have a potential future, but she's afraid to take that leap of faith. I still sense hesitation. *Shit.* I can't push her. I won't. She has to want this enough to overcome her fears, and she has to believe in us enough to take a risk. I learned from Ellie that a relationship is no good if only one person wants it.

"I understand."

"You're not going to tell me how stupid I was?"

"For being young and naive? No. You went to him openly and honestly—"

"Blindly."

"You have to forgive yourself for that. If you want to Monday-morning quarterback this thing, sure, maybe you should have seen the signs sooner. But the truth is, you shouldn't have had to. A grown-ass man should never have defiled a child, then strung her along for years before plotting to ruin her life and wash his hands. The fact he didn't give two shits about his own son or daughter you were having is just the cherry on top of his shit sundae."

"Oh, he offered me money to terminate the pregnancy. If I did, he'd write me a glowing recommendation for a future job. He had friends in all the right places, if I wanted to provide the same level of…service he was accustomed to. Suffice it to say I told him to shove his offer up his ass and slammed my way out of the office. I never saw him again."

Wishing I could inflict more violence on this fucking scum-sucking shitbag doesn't do anything to help the pensive woman in front of me barely holding back tears. Instead, I squeeze her hand. "Mandy, baby…"

"I expected that to be the end of it. I left Reed Financial that day, resolving to find another job as soon as possible and have my baby on my own. I devised a stupid story about a one-night stand with consequences for my dad and my brother. But the truth came out a couple of months after Oliver was born, when Barclay got arrested. My family dynamics have been a mess since."

I can only imagine. If they're blaming her—and at least Douglas Lund seems to be—they're idiots. But right now, my bigger concern is Mandy. "Are you still going to therapy?"

She nods. "It hasn't been easy. Celeste, my therapist, still thinks I blame myself more than I should."

"From what I've heard you say, I agree."

"I'm still trying to reconcile it all in my head, but I've made a lot of progress."

I bring her closer. "Good. But I hate that you believed his lies. He had to know what you were thinking."

"About our future? He did. He never corrected me, just hauled me back to bed. So…I'm a train wreck. I haven't had sex in way too long, and you're the only other man I've ever kissed. Aren't you sorry you ever thought you were interested?"

"Don't try to deflect me with sarcasm. I'm still interested." And I hate that she's mentally flinching, giving us both an excuse for me to walk away before I've even had the thought to. "It's going to take something far worse than the truth to shake me off, baby."

Her smile is one of the prettiest things I've ever seen, and more precious because I know it's real. "Why are you so understanding?"

"Did you ever stop to think that maybe you're just used to a complete asswipe, so any normal guy seems like a saint?"

"No. I've met plenty of perfectly nice guys, too. Bruce, for example. Not interested." She hesitates. "Couldn't trust him. I tried, but…no. You? I trust. I'm still trying to figure out why."

Just like I'm trying to figure out why I want Mandy so much. Not just sexually, though god knows that as we're both basically sitting here in our underwear, I wouldn't mind laying her back and making love to her. But I don't know where her head is, and I need more time to process everything she's told me. Though I'm not deciding about us. I've already done that. My heart knows, as crazy as that sounds.

I tuck a pale strand that worked free from her braid behind her ear. "Maybe we're both doing something we should have done years earlier. We're listening to our gut."

Her smile widens to something so pure she seems to glow. "Maybe you're right."

Then she hides a yawn behind her hand, stretches, and closes her eyes. "I'm so tired."

"Go back to sleep. I could use some extra z's, too. If you need anything, I'll be in the next room." I stand, grab my Glock, then palm her crown. "We'll worry about everything else later."

As I turn to leave, she grasps my hand and tugs me back. "Stay. Please."

"You're not ready for sex, Mandy. And that's not love."

She lifts her soft blue gaze to me, and it's a sucker punch to my chest. God, if I could wrap my arms around her and take away all her pain, I would right now. But doing anything else tonight would only confuse her more.

"You're right. But would you lie here and hold me?"

The hard outer shell of my resolve cracks. I lay my Glock on the nightstand again. "Of course."

"Thanks." She tugs me down to the bed until I'm flat on my back with my arm around her. She curls up to my side, resting her chin on my chest. "In case you hadn't figured it out yet, I think you're amazing."

"And I think you should stop buttering me up before I fall for you even more."

"Why would I want to stop that?"

Honestly, I'm not even sure I could if I wanted to. My heart feels as if I've pushed it over the cliff and it's now in free-fall. When it reaches the bottom, either Mandy will catch it…or it will shatter into too many pieces to put back together. I'm not sure which, but that doesn't stop me from holding her closer, kissing her forehead, and falling into a deep sleep beside her.

Chapter Eight

A few hours later, a light little giggle wakes me. What the hell?

Prying my eyes open, I look toward the sound—and find Mandy lying beside me. She's still wearing that champagne nightgown that arouses the fuck out of me. She has her head propped on her palm as she looks down at Oliver, who's between us laughing as his mother tickles his belly.

I can't help but smile. "Someone's in a good mood."

"Both of us. I haven't slept that well in months. Thank you."

"I didn't do anything except sleep, too." And probably deeper than someone hired to keep her safe should. "Feel better?"

"Much. Breakfast?"

"Coffee first. How long has Oliver been awake?"

"About forty-five minutes. I changed him, then we've been cuddling. Sorry if we woke you."

"Nope. I need to get up."

Baby giggling snags my attention again, and I turn to him. He's still grinning when he puts a little palm to my cheek. His feet kick as if he's excited, then he lets out a happy squeal.

The joy on his face tugs at my heart. In fact, the scene feels domestic. Normal. Touching. I'm hoping to be a part of Mandy's future, but that means I'll be a part of Oliver's, too. Maybe I'll even end up being the closest thing he has to a father. The realization brings both a cold sweat and a lump to my throat.

"Go ahead," she says. "I'll make coffee and get this little guy some breakfast."

With a groan, I haul myself out of bed, Glock in hand, and meander to the office and find my duffel bag. I toss on clean clothes, brush my teeth, and check my phone. Douglas Lund has already texted.

I've got a check for a hundred grand in my hand. Ready to tell me where to find Amanda?

I ignore his text. He doesn't deserve a prompt answer, and I don't need his shit—or his money. I'm focused on Mandy.

Instead, I plod to the kitchen, where the scent of java fills the air. Some country song plays from her phone. She hums along as she scrambles an egg for Oliver, who's playing on the floor at her feet. He clings to her ankle with one hand and a toy truck with the other. She's put a new braid in her long hair. She's fresh-faced and smiling as she slides his egg onto a paper plate, chops up a banana, then sits him in her lap at the nook table.

She looks relaxed. Happy, like she knows she's where she should be, which gives her a serenity she didn't have even twenty-four hours ago. I hope I'm part of the reason for that.

"Hey," I call out.

Mandy sends me a smile. "Hi. Coffee should be ready in a minute."

"Thanks. What's this song?"

"'Woman, Amen.' It's Dirks Bentley."

It's upbeat and on the happy side. As I listen, I find myself identifying more than I thought I could with a genre I usually consider twang. But the world definitely has a way of shaking your faith. Mandy and I have both been rattled by it. Then the singer croons something that, on the surface sounds silly, but might explain why I'm falling for her so quickly. Her feelings for me, even if they're new, are filling the cracks left in my heart. And I hope my love can do the same for hers after Barclay shattered it.

As the song rolls on, I agree that Mandy definitely renews my faith. I've been wondering if, after the divorce, I'd spend the rest of my life alone. But now I have hope. And I'll do whatever it takes to convince Mandy to stay with me. I want to be strong for her, and that gives me strength in return. So I'm waiting for her love, preferably without end. And if it all works out? Then I'll thank God for this woman, amen.

It's funny how the roads of my life have led me to her. So many circumstances—her break-up, my divorce, and the angry mob on her tail—have brought us to Maui, and along with a few chance meetings with mutual friends, together at this moment.

It's up to us to make it more.

"What should we do today?" she asks, interrupting my musing.

"Let's brush up on your self-defense, make sure you're able to defend yourself, just in case."

Her smile falters. "You mean in case I'm alone?"

Is she asking me in a roundabout way if I intend to leave her? I've been worried about her walking away and breaking my heart, so I haven't really laid my cards on the table. "Mandy, unless you tell me to get lost, the only way you're going to be alone is if something happens to me. But even in that situation, I want you to have a fighting chance."

"Thank you." She swallows. "I'm beginning to think I never want to be without you."

I don't care that Oliver is eating on her lap or that I really don't have a right. I cross the kitchen and cradle her face in my hands. "You're changing my life, baby, and I don't know what it will look like when we figure it all out. I just believe with everything inside me that we're here together for a reason, and I'm hoping that never changes."

Her smile turns even brighter. "I've been trying to keep you at arm's length…but I'm quickly running out of reasons I should."

That's all I needed to hear.

I bend and take her lips, sinking instantly into the softest, sweetest mouth I've ever kissed. She welcomes me, stroke for stroke, and she clings to me, feeling so perfect. No, she feels like home.

Between us, Oliver slaps his little palm on the table and squeals for attention. I pull back with a laugh. "Wanting some of Mom's attention, too, big guy?"

He grins, then plucks up his sippy cup and offers it to me.

"Oh, you must be special," Mandy proclaims. "I'm the only other person he's ever offered to share with. That means he likes you."

"Good. I like him, too." I kneel down to his level. "No offense, but I'm waiting for coffee. You'll understand when you're older."

Mandy smiles as she sets the sippy cup back on the kitchen table. "Finish your eggs, Oliver."

He ignores the spoonful she tries to choo-choo to his lips and instead blows me a kiss.

She rears back. "I've been trying to teach him that for weeks, and you're the first person he's done that to. He definitely likes you."

With a smile, I kiss the top of his head, then cup Mandy's face, thumbing my way across her cheek. "If things work out for us the way I hope, that will be a good thing."

Before she can respond, her phone chirps. She jumps up to retrieve the device. I hope it's not Bruce cluttering up her messages again. "Harlow wants to know if we'll come by. She can't leave since she's watching both her son and helping Noah's mother. Anyway, she wants to talk." Mandy turns pensive. "We haven't since she found out I was having an affair with her father. It would be nice to clear the air. I won't stay long. You know, to be on the safe side. But she also volunteered to watch Oliver for a bit. She wants the chance to get to know her baby brother. Maybe we could go shooting again?"

"Probably a good idea."

After some coffee, she makes a quick breakfast, then leaves me with Oliver, who's now half watching a cartoon on her iPad while playing with another of his toy trucks on the living room floor. I see my future. Not in this house, but here on Maui with Mandy and her son…and all his grown-up siblings who are having children of their own. I see opening a new range, being good friends with Trace. I picture his baby boy Ranger and Oliver growing up together. I even imagine having my own children with Mandy. I can almost taste how happy we'd be. And I want it so fucking bad.

First, I have to make this threat against her stop. I'm grateful last night was quiet so we could sleep and regroup. Now I want to figure out who this asshole is and end this mess.

How?

Mandy breezes out of the bedroom, now in another summery dress in a muted green and tan sandals. Her hair hangs loose to the small of her waist. She's applied some mascara that draws attention to her blue eyes and a hint of lip gloss that enhances her smile.

Could I really be lucky enough to spend the rest of my life with a woman this gorgeous, both inside and out?

"I'm ready."

I stand and pluck Oliver from the floor, grabbing one of his trucks for amusement when he fusses. "Let's go."

"I texted Harlow to thank her and tell her we're on our way."

Vaguely, I wonder if *the* Noah Weston will be there. I would like to meet him someday, but now is mostly about Mandy and Harlow patching up their friendship, not me celebrity gawking.

After a trip to the post office, Mandy holds my hand as I mail my divorce papers. Other than a formality, Ellie and I are over. It's the end of one part of my life. But a glance down at the beautiful blonde beside me makes me glad for the part I pray is about to start.

From there, GPS takes us to the swankiest part of the island, beyond a live guard and an electronic gate. I park the car, and Harlow stands outside in a red blouse and a pair of crisp white shorts, dark hair curling around her shoulders. Beside her is a hulk of a man who looks like an older version of Trace holding an infant.

Beside me, Mandy slides out of the Mustang, then frees Oliver from his car seat. Together they walk toward Harlow and Noah. I follow, hanging behind. I don't want to be in the middle of their reunion, but I should be close if she needs me.

"Hi," Mandy says to them.

I know that voice. I hear the hesitation in it. She's hopeful...but unsure of her welcome. She's aware of how much she screwed up the Reed family and she feels terrible.

"Good to see you." Harlow waves.

Mandy sends her a tentative smile. "Is it? You don't hate me?"

The brunette tsks. "I thought we'd get inside before we dove into the heavy stuff, but...what the hell? No, I don't hate you. I don't understand because I've always known my dad was an unfeeling, womanizing douche. And if I'd known you had a crush on him—"

"It was more than a crush."

Harlow's face softens. "Obviously. If I'd known, I would have told you the truth about him long before anything happened between you two. But"—she smiles brightly—"then we wouldn't have Oliver." She crouches and holds out her arms to the little boy.

I'm surprised when he goes right to her. When Harlow picks him up, their identical eyes make it obvious they're both Barclay Reed's kids.

"Nice to finally meet you," Mandy says to Noah.

"Likewise. I've heard a lot about you."

"Hopefully some of it was good." She's only half joking.

"Most. The rest? That's just Harlow being Harlow." He winks.

"That's always been true." Mandy manages a grin, looking a bit less tense.

"What?" Harlow shrugs. "I'm just slightly opinionated."

They both turn to her with astonished expressions. "Slightly?"

Laughing, I stick out my hand to Noah. "Tanner Kirk. It's an honor to meet you, Mr. Weston."

"Just Noah. Nice to meet you, too. Beer?"

I don't care that I'll have to restrict myself to a couple of sips. I'm talking to Noah freaking Weston. "That sounds great."

The women head inside the humongous oceanside mansion. It's like something out of a magazine, and I try not to gawk. Just...wow. Mandy seems unruffled by it all, which confirms again that she grew up uber wealthy. I still wonder what she's doing with me. I'm never going to be able to give her half of this luxury. On the other hand, she's had the slick, wealthy guy. I have to believe she'd ten times rather have something real. If that's what she wants, she's with the right man.

"Any preference?" Noah asks as he opens the fridge. "Trace subscribed me to some beer-of-the-month club for my birthday, so I've got a collection."

It's a little surreal that I'm standing in the kitchen of a future NFL Hall-of-Famer whom I've watched on TV many a past Sunday. But in person, he just seems like a typical dude. "I'm easy. Surprise me."

He shrugs and hands me a pale ale. According to the label, it's brewed in Belgium and has a pear flavor. It's not like anything I've ever had, but why not?

Noah lifts a similar bottle, this one flavored with grapefruit. "Cheers."

We clink bottles as the women gather on the far side of the expansive kitchen. "Cheers. Amazing place you've got."

"Maxon and Griff sold it to me. That's how I met Harlow. When I arrived on the island, she was housesitting—in a red bikini. How could I say no?"

I smile and sneak a glance over at Mandy. She and Harlow are talking quietly. I can't read either woman's face, but the conversation seems intense.

"So my brother tells me you're bodyguarding Amanda?"

I jerk my gaze back to him. "Yeah."

"Any trouble last night?"

"It was quiet." I glance at Mandy again, who now looks teary. It takes all my willpower not to cross the room and wrap a supportive arm around her. "Is Harlow going to forgive her?" Noah may tell me to fuck off...but I hope he won't. "It would mean the world to Mandy. She's been through a lot."

"Mandy, huh?" His glance is full of speculation. I ignore his unspoken question. "Yeah. My wife understands quite well what it means to be young and to fall for a player. She's not mad at Amanda. Did she hope that maybe the friend she's had her whole life would want to talk sooner? Invite her to meet her baby brother? Sure. But she's not so hurt that it will end their friendship unless Amanda wants it to."

I shake my head. "I think she'll be thrilled to spend time with Harlow once she knows she's welcome."

"We talked to Griff last night, and he told us about Amanda's apology. It gave Harlow hope that they could be friends again."

"Mandy would like that. I think she's going to move here."

"With you? Because the way you're looking at her, I'm thinking you're more than her bodyguard."

It's none of his business, but I'm betting that he and his wife could be allies. "I'd like to be, and she knows it."

"From what Harlow told me, Amanda needs and deserves someone who will be honest, faithful, and devoted to her. Can you be all that?"

"Yes, but the ball is in her court."

"Wrong sport for me…" Noah smiles. "But let me know if I can help."

"Harlow told Mandy you two would be willing to watch Oliver for a few hours. I know you've got your own baby and your mother and—"

"I've also got extra hands here today. Nia and her husband's best friend, Sebastian, are hosting some super-secret meeting for the executive management of Evan's company, Stratus, in our ohana out back. But they'll be breaking shortly. You looking to slip away for a romantic afternoon?"

It would be nice, but… "My primary goal is to get in more self-defense and target practice. Mandy is determined to learn how to defend herself when the need arises again."

"Sounds like a good idea. And if she's worried about Oliver's safety, there are five adults in this house, plus the guard outside. Trace should have told y'all to come here when the shit went down at Nia's place."

"Mandy will probably take you up on the offer to keep Oliver for a few hours, but she would refuse to stay here when she's a target. She doesn't want to bring trouble to you or anyone else she loves. I'm sure she appreciates the thought, but we're fine where we are."

"And I imagine you're more alone with her wherever you're staying than you would be here."

It wasn't my first thought, but… "Can't deny that."

Noah smiles, and I turn to see Mandy leaning in to hug Harlow. I'm proud of her because I know mending fences couldn't have been easy. She's clearly worried the Reed clan hated her for being a home wrecker, but they've all been kind and forgiving—unlike their father.

The pretty brunette smiles as she hugs Mandy back. "Want to come upstairs and meet Nolan?"

"I'd love to." She looks genuinely happy. "Stephen shared the pictures on social media with me. He looks amazing, so much like Noah. But he has your smile."

"He does. He's not even eight weeks old, and I can already tell he's going to be physical and athletic like his daddy." Harlow winks. "But he's got Mommy's attitude."

Mandy actually laughs. "Uh-oh. Watch out, world!"

"Right? We also have Trace's little boy, Ranger, with us for the night. He's going to be a pistol, too."

The women disappear upstairs with Oliver, and I can hear the cooing and the conversation echo across the tile floors.

Noah leans back against the nearest counter. "My mom will eat up having Oliver here. Now that Griff and Britta have announced they're having a third, she's all over Harlow and me to get busy again."

Already? "What does Harlow think?"

His smile turns all sly grin. "We're trying. I'd like two close together. Trace and I bonded a lot because we were. She wants a girl. But whatever happens, we're both happy."

I can tell. "Congratulations."

Suddenly, the back door opens. Nia charges in, shaking her head, then speaking over her shoulder at the buttoned-up suit following. "How the hell did you screw up everything before day one, Bas?"

"It's not like I went out of my way to nail the competition," he insists. "I was at a bar. She walked in. I flirted. She flirted back. Then—"

"I don't need a play-by-play." Nia wrinkles her nose. "But you literally had sex with the competitor who's trying to ruin our business."

"No, I had sex with a gorgeous redhead who flipped my switch. I didn't ask her for her life story before we fell into bed."

Nia turns and glares at him. "Did you even ask her name?"

He clams up. "I'm not apologizing for my sex life."

"At least admit that taking her to bed was a mistake." Bas is silent, irritating Nia even more. "How the hell are you supposed to lead the negotiation to buy her business out from under her? We all knew it would be messy since she's not inclined to sell, but how much more hostile will it be when she realizes you screwed her literally and figuratively?"

"She shouldn't be hostile after the number of orgasms I gave her."

"I'm going to pretend I didn't hear that." Nia cocks her hand on her hip. "When Evan hears about this, he'll be pissed."

"He, of all people, knows I need to move on."

I only have the vaguest idea what they're talking about, but Nia doesn't seem to be backing down. Neither is Bas. Competitor or not, I don't think he's done with this woman.

Noah clears his throat, and they both jolt as they realize they're not alone. "Hi."

"Sorry," Nia apologizes. "I didn't see you two there."

I don't know how they missed us since we're standing in the middle of the kitchen. She was probably too focused on reaming out Sebastian, and he was probably too busy defending himself.

"No worries," Noah assures. "Tanner, this is Sebastian Shaw. Bas, Tanner Kirk."

"Hey." The tall guy with blond hair in a precise corporate cut sticks out his hand. "Good to meet you."

"Likewise."

An uncomfortable silence falls then, like no one knows how to clear the air of Bas accidentally sleeping with the enemy.

"Well…I'll just go find a tall tree and hang myself." Bas sends Nia an acidic glance.

She tsks at him. "Dramatic much? We have to figure out how to fix this situation."

"Nia, she still doesn't know who I am…"

"You are *not* suggesting that you keep sleeping with her while the rest of us negotiate, I hope." Nia shakes her head as she refills her glass from the water dispenser on the fridge door. "Of course you are."

"Well, I can't exactly undo Saturday night, but I can try to get some, um…insider information."

"I'm definitely going to pretend I didn't hear that."

"You got a better idea?"

"No, but I didn't make the mess. You did. Fix it."

Then Nia marches for the back door again. Bas follows until they disappear out back, leaving silence in their wake.

"Well, he clearly stepped in shit," Noah quips.

"Yep, and I wouldn't want to be wearing his shoes."

We make a little more small talk about his new job color commentating for a network's NFL broadcasts, and I assure him he did an amazing job last season when he cocks his head my way. "So what do you do?"

"I'm a firearms instructor. Have been for seventeen years. Until recently, I owned a range in Colorado. I'd like to open one here. Got the place all staked out."

"What's your timeframe?"

How the hell do I explain to a guy who owns a twenty-five million dollar house that I'm short on cash? "Probably a couple of months. Nothing is set in stone yet. I've got to get a few things worked out and—"

"Would you have time to instruct a few of the security guards around here first?"

Is he serious? "You'd want me to?"

"Once you're done helping Amanda, yeah. Harlow and I have had our share of problems with people respecting our property lines and our privacy. No one dangerous…so far. But occasionally, paparazzi try to sneak around the place and get photos of us. Sometimes, it's a curious fan. When I hired the security team, I hoped that simply having guards would be deterrent enough, but these trespassers aren't letting up. Some are getting really bold. I'd like the security team to brush up, be both safe and proficient, before I put any weapons in their hands." He peers my way. "You any good at your job?"

"Damn good. I don't expect you to take my word for it, but—"

"My brother likes you. That counts a lot with me. And Amanda trusts you. I see it on her face. That's a feat. Based on what my wife has told me, the last couple of years Amanda cut nearly everyone out of her life—not just friends, but most of her family, too. She just doesn't let anyone close. Stephen has had to fight just to get her to take his calls."

"Granted, I don't know him, but the phone conversation we had? He behaved like an asswipe."

Noah laughs. "Do you have any siblings?"

"No," I admit.

"When you're the oldest, you feel as if it's your role to protect the younger ones, especially your sister. My sister Samaria had a couple of bullies back in grade school, who I realize now probably had crushes on her. But boy was I pissed that anyone was messing with my sister, and I would have totally punched their lights out if anyone had let me."

Protecting a kid, sure, but… "Stephen should be more mature than a grade-schooler."

"He is. Reserve judgment until you actually meet him. He's been concerned about Amanda. I think he was totally blindsided to find out that her boss, who was old enough to be her dad, had taken advantage of his position of power, coaxed her into bed, and gotten her pregnant."

I'm not telling Noah that wasn't the case since it's Mandy's secret. But if that's what Stephen believes, I can see how he might be worried I'll use our isolation and my close proximity to seduce her into another mistake. "Thanks for the info."

Noah smiles. "You still think he's an ass."

"He was that day. But I'll take a wait-and-see approach."

"Thanks. Since Amanda trusts you after everything she's been through, I'm guessing I can, too." He cocks his head. "If she's going to stay on the island, has she said anything about work? What kind is she looking for?"

That's a more difficult question. "I know she tried to find a job in LA, but after Barclay's arrest…"

Noah grimaces. "Listing her position as a felonious thief's executive assistant probably didn't look good on her resumé."

"Nope. And will it be any better on Maui?" I'm guessing not.

"Do you know if she's looking for another assistant job?"

I shake my head. "We haven't talked about it. Everything has happened so fast. We spent a lot of yesterday moving her to Masey's vacation rental. Then she and Oliver tried to recover from being awake half the night."

"I'm sure. The thing is, Harlow has been running our non-profit, the Weston Foundation, dedicated to helping athletes of all ages, from all over the country, who have suffered long-term injury as a result of concussions and other head trauma to get the resources they need. She's worked relentlessly to help everyone from children to pros get the right doctors, therapists, and facilities—not to mention the money—to rehabilitate."

"That sounds like a great cause."

"It is. We got to know each other because I suffered speech deficits after multiple concussions on the field, and she's a trained speech therapist. She helped me tremendously, but I know too many people don't know where to find the necessary resources and can't afford them if they do. Harlow has been the heart and soul of this organization from day one. Her last secretary got married and moved to Florida two weeks ago. My wife has been tearing her hair out since. Think Amanda might be interested?"

Would Harlow really want to hire the childhood friend who had an affair with her father? "I can't speak for Mandy, but I don't know of a reason she'd say no…except child care. Oliver—"

"Would be welcome to come with her every day. We've hired a nanny for Nolan, who starts next week. If Amanda would be willing to pay her some, too, I don't see why it wouldn't work."

It sounds pretty perfect. "Run it by your wife. If she's amenable, have her call Mandy and ask. Honestly, I think she'd be thrilled."

And in the space of ten minutes, a guy I just met but always admired on the field helped us both find income streams to get on our feet financially. And once my Colorado house sells, if Mandy will move in with me…we can start our future together.

If she's willing to spend the rest of her life with me. Right now, that's the big if.

A minute later, the women come down the stairs. After a little conversation, Mandy thanks Harlow and Noah profusely for agreeing to keep Oliver.

Once she gives Harlow the diaper bag and kisses the boy's head, I take her hand and lead her to the door. "Thanks. We'll be back once we've managed more target practice. A couple of hours at most."

"Don't hurry," Noah assures. "Why don't you come back around six? We can all have dinner then."

I turn to Mandy, but she's already smiling. "That would be great. Thank you both."

Then we're gone, heading back to the indoor range we visited yesterday.

"That went well," I say.

A happy smile flits across her face. "Yeah. Harlow has always been the sister I didn't have, and it hurt me so much to think she might never speak to me again because of my stupid choices."

"According to Noah, she's missed you, too."

"She told me." Mandy's smile widens. "It was great to see her again. It felt like we had never been apart."

I don't mention the jobs Noah and I discussed. If Harlow is willing to hire Mandy, that should come from her.

At the range, I rent Mandy two different guns and let her fire mine. She's much less hesitant and a lot more confident than yesterday. I don't even have to instruct her; she simply loads both the new revolver and the semiautomatic's magazine. With ammo in place on each, she fires away at the targets, hitting her paper intruder a lot more, some shots even dead center.

"You did great," I say as we head back to the Mustang.

"It feels good. I'm actually believing that I could defend Oliver and myself if I had to. Hopefully, I won't." Once we slide into the car, Mandy reaches for my hand. "Thank you for this morning. For listening and not judging me too harshly. I'm not convinced my family would be half so understanding."

"But they don't know the truth?"

She shakes her head. "They don't."

I scowl as I stop at a red light. "Why not tell them?"

"Honestly? I don't think I could stand the disappointment on my dad's face. I always wanted to be a daddy's girl...and he wasn't interested."

With one sentence, the pieces of the puzzle come together. "You gravitated to Barclay because you could feel both like a daddy's girl and a woman."

She winces. "That sounds really messed up, doesn't it?"

"It sounds human, baby. No one is perfect, and anyone who you tells you differently is selling something."

"Probably."

"I think you should level with your family. You're hiding here and—"

"I don't want to move back to New York."

"Fair enough. But they're still your family. They might understand a lot more than you think."

She's quiet for a long minute. "I'll think about it. Where are you taking me?"

"Lunch?"

"Please. I'm starved."

We find our way to a little café known for its homemade soups and breads and munch on a quick bite. Mandy isn't saying much, but the way she keeps looking at me grips me by the throat. She's got something on her mind, and I have a suspicion it's big.

"Out with it," I demand. "What are you thinking?"

"Why do you assume I'm thinking anything?" But her secretive half smile reaffirms that she is.

I raise a brow. If she wants to play that game, fine. I'll play along...for now. "Anywhere else you want to go? We don't have to be back to Noah and Harlow's for about five hours."

"To the villa?"

I'm not sure what she's up to, but I shrug. "If you want."

The ride there is quiet, but I sense her thoughts still churning. It's fucking with my head.

By the time I pull into the garage, close the massive door behind us, and climb out of the car, the air between us pings with tension.

Inside, she pulls her phone from her purse, checks it, then sets it aside. "I should do laundry."

"Or we could brush up on your self-defense."

"We could, but..." She draws in a deep breath. "Tanner, I told you I'd give us some thought, and I have. You've protected me even when you knew I couldn't pay you right away. You listened to me. You didn't judge me. You've supported me. You've been everything I wanted Barclay to be, only better. While we should maybe see to other responsibilities, and we can if that's what you want, but I'd rather you kiss me again...and maybe not stop this time."

Chapter Nine

My heart starts revving instantly. I swallow back my excitement enough to ask the right questions. "You have no idea how much I want to, baby. Are you sure?"

She crosses her arms over her chest. Through the nearby window, the sun slants in, lighting her blond hair with a halo and illuminating her skin with a glow. But she's more than beautiful to me. It's somehow sexy that, despite not having known her long, I know her truth—and the real her—probably better than anyone else.

"Are you worried I'm repeating my history or making the same mistake again?"

I don't think so, but I want to make sure I understand. "What do you mean?"

"Well, here I am again, throwing myself at an older man who—"

"Stop there. First of all, you're not throwing yourself at me; we're talking together about the possibility of taking a forward step in our relationship, like adults. And that's the second distinction. You're an *adult* now. You understand what sex is and the ramifications of it. So to answer your question, no, I don't think you're making the same mistake again. I'm older than you, sure. But not old enough to be your father. And I'd never want to replace him in any way."

"I wouldn't want you to. My dad and I have always had a complicated relationship, and we have to work that out. But my brother telling you I need a 'daddy' is his oversimplification of my desire to have the kind of man in my life who will protect me."

"I'll do more than protect you, baby. Give me a little time, and I'm convinced that nothing will stop me from falling in love with you."

She sends me a tremulous smile as tears tremble on her lashes. "Give me time, and I don't think I'll be able to stop myself from falling in love with you, either."

Once I hear that, I can't keep my hands off her anymore, so I wrap one palm around her nape. The other hand filters through the silken strands of her hair. "Does that mean you've thought more about us?"

She lays her hands on my shoulders and sways closer, nodding. "That's why I told you to kiss me."

"You also said not to stop. So that's a yes?" I fuse my gaze to hers. "I want to be very clear."

"I know, and that's another reason I don't think I can stop myself from falling in love. You're honest and honorable. And you're ridiculously hot." She laughs at herself. "Even if we're crazy for thinking we can build a future together after knowing each other for a couple of days, I don't care. It feels right."

"It does to me, too. So...we're doing this?"

"This?" She raises a brow. "If you mean sex, hopefully that's a given."

I chuckle. "It is. But I meant life."

"Let's try. I just don't know how good I'll be at it. I've never tried to spend my life with anyone."

"Hey, I have, and it didn't end well." I shrug. "Maybe I'll suck at it again."

"Or we'll learn together." She presses closer. "You always try to make me feel better. I can't tell you how much that means to me."

"The person you spend your life with should." I caress her cheek, my work-roughened palm skimming her skin. "But I have to be honest, Mandy. Life with me won't be luxurious. I know you're used to—"

"I'm used to everyone in my life with money assuming they can use it to bend me to their will, and I'm sick and tired of it. Whatever we have, we'll earn together. That will mean far more to me than gold bathroom fixtures and trips to Paris."

I love her outlook. "Are you saying the French are overrated?"

She grimaces. "Actually, Paris is one of the most beautiful cities in the world, and I'll miss it. But I don't need it the way I need you."

"Oh, baby, I need you, too." I step closer again—and drop one hand to the strap of her summery dress. "I need to see you, feel you, sink into you."

She closes her eyes. "Yes."

"I need to feel like you're mine."

"I want that."

I slide my fingers under her strap and slowly lift it off her shoulder. When I drop it, the thin strip of fabric hangs halfway down her arm. "Your first time was hurried." Not to mention painful. "I want ours to be different, and we have all afternoon."

Mandy's cheeks bloom with color. "I'd love that."

"Come with me." I hold out my hand.

She takes it without hesitation. I lead her to the big master bedroom overlooking the ocean and the mostly private beach. Even here the sun shines on her like she's an angel. I feel so lucky that I'll have her in my arms.

"This is going to be intense, isn't it?"

With chemistry like ours? "Yeah."

I've intentionally blocked as many sexual thoughts of Mandy as I could. But now that she's removed my mental barrier, a million lascivious thoughts flood my brain. But first, she asked me to kiss her.

When I bend to her, she's already waiting for me, eyes closed trustingly, lips soft and waiting. My blood surges, and I eliminate the distance between us until I lay my mouth over hers. She opens to me. Her sugary lips meld against mine as she moans. She's the sweetest thing I've ever tasted.

My fingers tighten around her nape as I nudge her open wider and kiss her deeper. Then I use my other hand to lower the remaining strap from her other shoulder. I'm reluctant to break the kiss and leave her mouth, but I need to look into her eyes, study her...peer into her soul. Is she really ready for what's next?

Her baby blues have gone darker. They're full of invitation.

Yes, she's ready.

And her damn cotton dress is barely clinging to the swells of her breasts. One deep breath, and I'll be able to see everything it's concealing.

I swallow. "Mandy..."

"Don't stop there." Her breaths sound rougher. "I need your hands on me, Tanner."

Oh, I'll be putting my mouth everywhere, too. "Nice and slow, baby. I want to give you the first time you should have had."

Something more than acceptance crosses her face. It looks like need. And gratitude. That's what I'm seeing. Her expression is so soft and angelic…but I see the hint of something devilish there, too.

My heart thumps as I lift my hand to the fabric straining between her breasts—then give it a tug.

The cotton slides down, exposing a strapless something lacy that's not quite a bra. It adheres to her curves, but I can see straight through it. Her taut pink nipples nearly make me swallow my tongue.

Somehow, I manage to tear my stare away and back to her face. "Oh, baby…"

"I'll get rid of this." She reaches behind her back to unclasp the transparent scrap of undergarment.

Gently, I grab her wrists. "Let me."

With a nod, she releases the band, then slides her palms up my arms to my shoulders, closing her eyes, giving herself over. That's even sexier, the trust she's placing in me. I'm so damn hard that my first impulse is to toss her on the bed, cover her body with mine, and shove my way inside her. But there will be time for that later. Now is about her. It's about building us.

I bend and brush my lips up her neck as I work the clasps open at the small of her back. It falls away as I lift her chin to me and seize her lips. Mandy is soft and open again, this time welcoming me with passion, too. My other hand glides down her body, pausing to cradle her breast and thumb her taut nipple. As she gasps and clings tighter, I skim down to her hip, settling my hand under her dress, then begin to peel it away until it falls to her ankles.

I'm so damn torn. I want to keep kissing her sweet mouth, dive even deeper into it while reveling in every catch of her breath, at the same time I want to relish every inch of her smooth, pearly skin I just revealed.

Mandy makes the decision for me when she eases away from our kiss with heavy-lidded eyes and kicks off her shoes. Then she stands before me, and I can hardly breathe. She's not perfect, but she's so damn female and lush. And she's nearly heart-poundingly bare. Visually, I follow the lean line of her naked torso from the hint of her ribs, swoop into the soft curve of her waist, then out again to the jut of her hips where her small white lace panties cling. The neat little bow in the middle of the band, flirting so deliciously close to her pussy, nearly makes me lose my mind.

"You're staring. I know I've still got an extra ten pounds I can't seem to lose after Oliver."

I lay a finger over her lips. "You don't need to. You're beautiful. I love that you have breasts just the right size to nestle into my palms." As I cup them both, I drop a kiss to her shoulder. "And I love that you have hips and thighs I'll be able to wrap my hands around."

"And I have plenty of ass," she quips.

I smile as I spin her around and drop my stare. My mouth goes dry. My palms clutch her. "Which fills my hands perfectly, too. I'm going to love hanging on to this while I'm on top of you, driving you to orgasm."

She shudders as I turn her to face me again. "I want that."

"I want to make you feel good." About her choice, her body, and her sexuality. About us.

Mandy skates her palm up my chest and wraps her arms around my neck. "I want to make you feel good, too. Tell me what you like."

"You. Everything about you. Let's not analyze this, baby. Let's just let it happen, okay?"

She nods. "Okay, but you're overdressed."

I'm fully dressed, and that's by design. If my clothes start coming off now, things will heat up too quickly. Instinct tells me not to rush her. Barclay never appreciated her or savored her. I refuse to make his mistake because I'm too impatient.

"I'll get naked when the time is right. Now…" I drop my hands to her hips and start easing her panties down her thighs.

When they reach her ankles, she steps out and kicks them away. I hear her swallow.

There's a thin dusting of light brown hair shielding her naked pussy. I gape at how gorgeous she is everywhere, but here in particular. She's pink and plump and juicy. Swollen. Aroused, despite the fact I've barely touched her.

"This…" I cup her mound in my hand. "This is where I want my mouth."

Her breath catches. "Please."

She begs sweetly. That kind of thing has never turned me on before. But now? My blood is firing. I'm itching to get my hands all over her. My mouth is watering for a taste.

Maybe as time goes on, I really am getting more caveman. Or maybe I'm finally realizing what I've wanted all along—someone soft and sweet who sees sex as a celebration of us. And maybe I'm finally admitting who I am now that I've found someone who appreciates that I'm all man.

"Open for me." I swipe my thumb across her bottom lip.

Mandy complies as her lashes flutter shut. I dip my head, cover her mouth...and lose myself in her sweetness. She wraps her arms around my neck and presses her body against me, lighting me up even more. Thank god the bed is right behind her, and all I have to do is guide her down to it.

She tumbles back softly, never breaking our kiss. But I need to make sure she's fully with me, so I lift my head and brush skeins of her pale hair from her face. "Baby?"

"I want you."

I kiss her throat, her cheeks, her forehead, breathing her in all the while. Then her mouth lures me back, and I cover it with mine, addicted to her honeyed flavor. As I sink into our kiss, she clings tighter. Her breath picks up pace. She arches up, and her legs part beneath me.

Holy hell.

"I'm trying to take this slow."

"I know and I appreciate it." She nips at my bottom lip as she wraps one of her thighs around my leg. "But I want you now. I've been without you all my life, and I need to make up for lost time."

She's right. That fact hits me between the eyes. Every moment of every day we have is precious, and we've both wasted years on dead ends. Our future starts now.

"Mandy, baby, I'm going to love you..." I tear my shirt over my head and toss it across the room.

Pressing my bare chest to hers is so electric. The sizzle ripples through my whole body and burns me. Passion grips me by the throat. I seize her mouth, stroking her with my tongue as I let my hands wander her body, worshipping her small waist before gripping her hips and lifting her up against my aching cock.

She tears her lips free with a groan, tossing her head back with a whimper. "Tanner..."

As she exposes her throat to me, I claim every inch of her skin with my kiss, then work my way to her collarbones, drift down to the upper swells of her breasts...until I'm hovering over one of her peaked nipples. "I'm going to suck this into my mouth."

"Yes."

"Hard. I'm going to lick it and prod it and drag it deep."

"Please," she pants.

"Then I'll start all over, until you feel the stroke of my mouth all the way through your body."

"Hurry."

Then her nails are in my shoulders, urging me on. My body keeps taking over, squeezing her hips and pressing my khaki-covered erection against her pussy. In response, she breathes harder—and parts her legs wider.

Fuck, this is getting hot fast. But she opened the door to our passion, and now I can't close it. I can't pretend that I don't need to light her on fire. I can't not wish like fuck that I was already inside her.

Then I do exactly what I spelled out. I dip my head and all but inhale her nipple. It's taut and gets even harder the moment my lips surround it. My tongue follows, curling, swirling, prodding and licking until her cheeks pinken. Until her breathing sounds choppy. Until she's undulating beneath me and silently begging for more.

When I pull back, she gasps in protest and tightens her leg around me. "No!"

"Shh. Yes," I insist as I dip my head to her other nipple and draw it into my mouth.

As I pull deep, Mandy arches. A moan escapes her lips. Then she melts back into the bed. "Yes…"

I focus on the first nipple again, relishing every sigh, cry, and whimper until her fingertips wander my body, until her hips wriggle restlessly, until I feel her heart beating furiously against mine.

Then I start making my way down her body, dragging my lips over the plane of her stomach. Her workout efforts are obvious, but so is her softness. The signs pregnancy left on her body somehow arouse me more, maybe because it's obvious she's fertile. I can't deny that the idea of her growing our children inside her does something to me. It's not purely sexual, though that idea turns me on. But it's about knowing we'd be tangling our blood, hearts, and lives to create the next generation we would raise on love.

Fuck, I'm getting awfully philosophical for a man about to get a first taste of his woman's pussy, but when I lower my shoulders between her thighs and her nails find their way to my scalp, the desire to make that a reality overwhelms me. So I focus on the here and now, loving the way she doesn't try to hide her need for me. She simply pulls me closer, opens for me more, and gives a long, high-pitched cry as my tongue swipes up her furrow before settling over her clit.

"Tanner!"

Everything about her response lights me on fire, especially the way she wants me. I part her with my thumbs and open her, tasting her again, drawing in her hidden sweetness. Then I try to press a pair of fingers inside her, finagling and working the digits into her tight, clenched cunt until she finally lets me in.

"How long has it been?"

She opens her eyes enough for me to see the uncertainty. "More than a year and a half."

Since she discovered she was pregnant with Oliver.

I keep sliding my fingers through her tight flesh, stroking, working, softening. "It's going to be good. I promise."

"It already is," she keens.

Smiling, I taste her again, lingering, savoring, loving her essence on my tongue and her cries in my ears. Minutes slide by as I lose myself in everything Mandy, bringing her up slowly until she's tensing, her thighs trembling, her breathing heavy.

"Tanner…"

"Baby," I murmur against her pussy. "You're so sweet."

"Please."

The sight of her fist bunched around the blanket and the rosy hue of arousal spreading up her chest tells me she's close. "What do you feel?"

"It's… I can't…" She gasps when I swirl my tongue around her again. "Oh, my god."

I keep licking her, from her entrance to her clit, lingering over the sensitive button, then rub it mercilessly with my thumb. "This pussy is mine."

"Yes."

"You're mine."

"Yes."

"You'll give me more whenever I want it."

"Yes." She nods emphatically. "I will. I promise."

No denying I've wanted sex—but I need Mandy. She's strong enough to take care of herself and her son when she needs to…but soft enough to let me take care of her when I crave it.

How can I not reward that?

I drag her clit into my mouth and suck it before lashing it with my tongue again. I don't relent until she stiffens, clutches me tight, and releases.

When the pleasure hits, her eyes clench shut. She wails out a strangled cry. Her entire body ripples and shudders with satisfaction. Then a fine sheen of perspiration covers her. A rosy flush consumes her skin. And she flops back to the mattress, boneless, panting…and smiling.

"Wow."

"I need you, Mandy." She's the only cure for my fever, and if I don't get inside her soon, I'll burn alive.

As she licks her lips, she nods earnestly—then spreads her legs wider. "I don't want to wait anymore. I'm here."

"You on the pill?" I attack the zipper of my shorts.

"No."

I'm not surprised, just momentarily frustrated that I can't simply work my way inside her and stroke us both to mutual screaming orgasm. But her not being on the pill now means she'll get pregnant more quickly once we've committed to each other and found an even financial footing.

With a nod, I withdraw the box of condoms I slipped into the nightstand drawer earlier and tear into it. I stand just long enough to kick my shorts and boxers aside, then roll on the latex. Then I'm back on the bed, scooping her thighs up in my arms and covering her body with my own as I probe her slick, swollen opening.

She's tight, but the rest of her is relaxed and open to me as I hold her legs apart. So slowly my teeth grit, she gives way to me an excruciating inch at a time. When she tenses and her breath hitches, I stop, ease back, then slowly inch forward again. Over and over. It seems to take forever to submerge my length inside her, but finally I push my cock deep, all the way to the base.

It's unlike anything I've ever felt, and a long, low groan slips from my throat.

Mandy lets out a breathy sigh and stares up at me with eyes so blue they seem to glow. "Oh, my god."

"You feel so good." I inch out and glide back in, smooth and easy. "Any pain?"

"It stings—in a good way. Like you're stretching me."

I press my hips forward, penetrating her even deeper. "Now?"

She gasps, then wriggles on me with a shake of her head. "No. It's so good. Do that again. You're hitting some spot inside me…"

Yeah, I am. I feel her enveloping me, closing and squeezing me tight. My sensitive head bumps and brushes against something that adds another tingle down my spine.

It's great, but I want more.

Grabbing one of the bed pillows, I settle it under her backside, lifting her hips.

"What are you doing?" she asks.

I don't explain. I just let our bodies do the talking, tipping her hips up even more—then I drive straight down.

"Oh!" She blinks at me, gaping. When I do it again, she lets out another breathy moan. "Yes. More…"

"Wrap your legs around me, Mandy."

She complies, and with my hands free I slide my palms up her arms until I'm tangling her fingers with my own. I press our foreheads together and close my eyes, stroking her deep and slow.

Everything about our joining is so intimate. I feel her everywhere—under me, clenching me, hugging me, gripping for dear life. I smell her scent, that hint of flowers that always seems to waft around her. I feel her harsh, steady breaths on my lips. More important, I feel her wonder and her pleasure so deeply I swear I can feel her soul, too.

"Tanner…"

"What do you need?"

Under me, she writhes. "Faster."

"Not yet."

"But I need… It burns."

She's right; I feel it, too. Just like I feel her tightening around me. "Let it build."

"But—"

I cut off her protest with a kiss, diving every bit as deep into her mouth as I do into her pussy. Then I settle into a slow, driving rhythm, relishing the feel of her clinging all around me and the sounds of her passion rising.

Soon, her tongue seeks mine as her hips lift to me. Under me, she's hot, like she's burning with fever. Her fingers grip my hands even tighter, her nails beginning to dig in. Then her breathing stutters. Her breaths become a mix of pants and whimpers. Her thighs tighten on me.

Yeah, she's close again. And thank fuck because I don't know how much longer I can hold out when she feels this damn good.

Mandy tears her mouth free. "Tanner, please!"

"Still burning, baby?"

She nods emphatically. "I need it. It's never been… I've never felt…oh, this. Yes."

"That's it. Almost there, and it's going to be so good."

I know that because sensations are skittering down my spine. The same burn she's fighting heats my blood and fires the rest of me. This orgasm is building, steadily, quickly, monumentally. When it comes, it's going to blow away every notion I've ever had of pleasure and leave me wanting only Mandy. I'll do anything—everything—to have her under me, open to me, and crying out for me for the rest of my life.

"Tanner. I'm begging. Please!"

"And god, I love it." I ease back on the depth and pace of my strokes, holding her orgasm hostage just a bit longer. "Give me more, baby…and I'll give you more."

Her gaze tangles with mine. Desperation lights her eyes. Her body undulates beneath me. Despite the fact she's biting her lush lower lip, she still can't hold all her whimpers in. "You can't leave me like this. I just need…"

"A little more?"

"Yes." Her fingernails dig deeper into my hand. "Yes. Please…"

I love hearing her plead. Maybe that means I'm messed up or something, but hearing Mandy beg for more of me and my touch does amazing things to my libido. I haven't felt really wanted in years. Ellie's sex drive definitely fell off a cliff once she realized there would be no children, and I haven't let myself be this intimately involved in someone's pleasure since. Sure, we fucked. But it was nothing like this. What I'm sharing now with Mandy is unlike anything I've imagined or felt.

Sliding my cheek against hers, I press my lips to her ear, then ease deep inside her again. "Fuck, your begging turns me on."

"Please…"

Her next words devolve into whimpers. She tries to wrap her arms around me, but I hold her down. She can't distract me now. I want her to feel every sensation I'm dying to give her.

Our stares meet again, and I fuse them together as I stretch our joined hands high above her head and press her into the mattress. Slowly, I withdraw again, this time almost completely.

"No. No… No! You can't—" More whimpers ensue and her skin turns rosier.

She's right on the edge. I feel her clenching on me tighter than ever. I hear it in her breathing. It's clear from her keening need.

I love ramping Mandy up and keeping her on edge. I have a feeling this is something I'll want to do to her again and again, not only for the sheer mind-fuck, but because I know it's going to make her orgasm cataclysmic. That's worth all the suffering on my end, too.

But I can't hold out much longer, not when everything about her is undoing me so utterly.

"I won't stop," I assure her with gritted teeth. "You want more? Harder? Now?"

"Yes!" She grinds up against me. "Yes. Now!"

"Baby…" I release her hands and clamp them around her hips, moving her with me stroke for stroke as I pick up the pace to something pounding and swift.

Her eyes widen. Her nails dig into my back. Her pussy tightens. The bed shakes and moans. Then she lets loose a sharp, hoarse cry as her entire body jolts and shudders under me.

It's the sexiest thing I've ever experienced—and there's no way I can stave off the ecstasy mainlining through my veins and setting every cell and nerve ending ablaze. The orgasm hits next, felling me with a sucker punch of satisfaction that rips away all control and leaves me shaking in the aftermath of something too incredible to name.

Beneath me, Mandy can't seem to catch her breath, but she still finds a way to worship me with her soft, sweet lips across my shoulder and up my neck before she's pressing a soft, exhausted buss against my mouth.

"Oh, wow…" she pants out. "I've never felt anything… I had no idea."

"Same." I manage to prop myself up on unsteady arms, despite feeling totally like a noodle. "That was amazing."

"Beyond."

I turn to look at the clock on the nightstand. "We've got over three hours before we have to pick Oliver up. Should we do that again?"

Mandy sends me a loopy grin. "Can you?"

Reluctantly, I pull from the heaven of her pussy and rise to trash my condom. As I turn and head back to the bed, I imagine having her on top of me, being deep, deep inside of her and watching her breasts bounce and jiggle as I wring multiple orgasms from her, then flipping her onto all fours and fucking her from behind until she begs for mercy I don't have. By the time I reach her, I'm hard as steel again.

I grab another condom. "I can if you can."

Her smile widens as she spreads herself open for me in invitation. "Yes, please."

After donning the latex, I plunge inside her again. As she gasps, I roll to my back, taking her with me, and positioning her on top. "You set the pace this time."

She does, and it's slow as molasses. Holy fuck, she's going to undo me—and I'm going to love it.

"You feel incredible," she pants out. "I want to do this with you forever."

With a fist in her hair, I urge her down until our faces are inches apart. "That's the plan, baby."

Chapter Ten

We stayed in bed the entire afternoon, indulging in a third round of lovemaking, before finally forcing ourselves apart with a last, lingering kiss. We showered until the water ran cold, then hustled into our clothes and out the door before heading back to Harlow and Noah's place.

When we arrive, Oliver and Ranger are playing happily with a mountain of toys while Nolan sleeps on a blanket nearby. Noah's mother regards the boys with an indulgent smile. It's obvious she loves being around the kids and is happy to play grandma.

After a tasty dinner with a lot of laughter, Nia and Sebastian drift into an office area downstairs and continue debating how to fix Sebastian's "mistake."

Harlow pulls Mandy aside, and they head out by the pool, each with their sons, for a chat. Noah's mother decides to give Ranger a bath upstairs.

That leaves me with Noah, who suggests a beer and a baseball game on the big screen.

Once we're seated and watching a replay of the Blue Jays beating the Orioles, we pop open our beers. Noah doesn't waste any time getting to the point. "When can you start training my security staff?"

"As soon as I put a stop to Amanda's would-be stalker." The mob will eventually go away. "I just wish I knew who the hell it was."

"You have nothing to go on?"

I shake my head. "She can't think of anyone in her life who would go this far to hurt her, and she's convinced it's somehow related to Barclay Reed."

"That wouldn't surprise me."

"Did you ever meet him?"

"Once." From Noah's expression, I know it wasn't pleasant.

I'm compelled to know as much as I can about the asshole who broke Mandy's heart. But there's also a chance he'll know something about Reed that will set me down the right path. "And?"

"I only needed thirty seconds to know that my wife was better off without him. That was my wedding gift to her, you know? I gave her parents three million dollars to get out of her life forever."

Holy shit. "Seriously?"

"One hundred percent."

"And they took it?"

"Linda jumped on it. She wanted to divorce the bastard and needed the money. Barclay was more reluctant, so I threatened to expose his affairs and illegitimate children—at least the ones I knew about—which I discovered during a deep dive into his life. Mind you, I discovered all this before it became public knowledge, but once I confronted him with the truth he fell in line."

I lean in since I don't want Mandy or anyone else to hear. "Was the information you gathered really bad?"

"Stomach-turning. We think he paid his former assistants' paternity claims under the table, which is why we can't locate the rest of those offspring now. But apparently, he shuffled in a new assistant about every two years, upgrading to a younger model...and repeated the cycle. It was an open secret at Reed Financial."

"Jesus."

"I don't know how many more illegitimate Reeds there are."

"Any chance one of them might be after Mandy?"

Noah shrugs. "It's possible someone might resent Amanda."

In theory, yes. But my gut keeps saying no.

"Look..." Noah says. "I know Reed did a number on Amanda—"

"You have no idea."

"Did she tell you?"

"Yeah. Stomach-turning, just like you said."

"Fuck. I'm sorry." He sighs. "I hope she'll tell Harlow someday, just like I hope my wife will tell Amanda what Reed did to her."

"Did he molest her?" I'm horrified by the possibility.

"No, but it was almost equally despicable. Now that I have a child of my own, I can't imagine using him as a pawn in some scheme simply to make myself richer."

"I don't know if Mandy would want to tell Harlow what her father did."

"I think it could bring them both closer together and help heal them someday."

Maybe he's right. I don't know.

"I'll get you the list of Reed's known assistants, along with my private investigator's notes about how many have children old enough to cause Mandy problems."

If any of them have the Reed eyes, their paternity would be a dead giveaway. "That would be great."

"I'll get it to you in the morning."

"Thanks."

"My pleasure. Let me know when you're free to start with my security staff. If you could work with them for a couple of months, would fifty thousand be fair?"

Beyond fair, and he must know it. "That's more than generous. I don't need that much money to do the job."

"Would you do it right?"

"Absolutely. I'll shoot for perfection, but at the very least they'll be well above competent."

"Then that's the offer, take it or leave it." He shrugs and sips his beer.

"Why are you helping me?"

"Two reasons. You seem like a good guy, and the fact you just tried to take less money for a job proves it. But even more important, my wife wants her friend back. Since you've come onto the scene, she says Amanda seems more like herself than she has been since she was a kid. I have to think that's your doing."

I fucking hope so. "Thanks. I won't let you down."

"I know. What's next for you and Amanda?"

"Catching whoever the hell is after her. Then…hopefully convincing her we have a future."

"Good luck. By the way, I think Harlow is offering her a job now."

As if those were the magic words, the back door opens, and the women enter, each carrying a squirming baby boy. I don't know Harlow's expressions well, but I can tell Mandy has been crying. Since she's smiling too, I'm hoping they're happy tears.

"Baby?" I stand.

She approaches me, smile widening. "I'm going to start working for Harlow next week. I have a lot of skills that she could use, and it's for a great cause."

"That's fantastic." I curl my arm around her waist. "Congratulations."

"It's such a relief. I didn't think I'd find another job with my employment history."

"And best of all, her new boss will never expect her to put out," Harlow quips.

Even Mandy laughs. "Thank goodness."

With that, we leave and head to the villa. Everything Noah told me lingers in the back of my brain. I wish I could get started on hunting down this scumbag tonight, but without his information and without any other leads, I'm stuck. But the hours between now and dawn won't be wasted. I'll have Mandy. And even though I've had her so much today I should be well sated, I'm not. I don't feel thirty-eight. I feel easily twenty years younger and I want more.

"Good conversation with Harlow?" I ask.

"Actually? Yeah. I started pulling away from her during our teen years. I felt so guilty about sleeping with her dad, but not enough to stop, which only made me feel worse. But she actually understood."

"You told her everything?"

"The highlights. But she knows how old I was when it started." A teasing grin dances at Mandy's mouth. "Harlow says if she had known she would have gleefully castrated the bastard herself."

Too bad no one did. "At least you cleared the air."

"Absolutely. We got some good truths between us, and then we talked for a few minutes. It felt like old times, but better. She's really happy, and I'm thrilled for her."

"Is that what happiness looks like to you?"

"What do you mean?"

"Big house, high-powered job…"

"No. She's happy because she's got a great husband, a precious son, and family all around." She shrugs. "I don't care about the house and the job nearly as much as I care about the people in my life. I'm hoping that will be you."

I take her hand. "After today, I don't know how you'll ever get rid of me."

Peace settles between us, along with an anticipation that hums just under the surface. We're both in a good place…mostly. We're looking forward to the future. And we can't wait to get Oliver down so we can hit the sheets again. But until then, I should give more thought to Mandy's assailant.

While I'm at it, I'll have to address the multitude of messages Douglas Lund has sent me since this morning, each more pissed off than the last. Clearly, he doesn't like being ignored. My silence should have told him I have zero intention of letting him know where I'm secreting his daughter. His insistence makes me wonder if Lund orchestrated the angry mob and the intruder to make some fucked-up point. After all, how many others really know that both Nia and Evan are branches on Mandy's complicated family tree?

By the time we reach the villa, Oliver is half asleep, so Mandy gives him a quick bath and a change, then sings him to sleep. I smile, listening from the hall. The deep love she's expressing is something I want for the rest of our lives.

In my hand, my phone buzzes. Lund Senior. Again.

Last chance or I'm tearing up this check. Where is my daughter?

Mentally, I start composing a reply, but I can't think of one that doesn't start and end with four-letter words. I've always disliked entitled pricks who are convinced their money should buy my obedience. I don't roll that way, and he can kiss my ass.

"You okay?" Mandy asks, suddenly right in front of me.

She finally seemed relaxed, even happy, this afternoon. I don't want to burden her with this now. Her father isn't something I can't handle. If Mandy and I work everything out, he might be my father-in-law. But that doesn't mean I'm going to pander to him. She will be my first responsibility and priority, so I'll do whatever it takes to shield her from his bullying and his attempts to control her.

I shuttle my messages, darken my phone, and shove it in my pocket. Lund can fucking wait—and he can shove his check, too. That means I'll have to delay opening the new range for an extra few months more than likely. The location might be rented by then. But somehow, I'll work it out. Mandy is worth it. "Yeah. Oliver down?"

"He's fighting sleep, but he's exhausted. Playing takes it out of a kid." She drags her fingers down my chest, straight to my belt buckle, curling her fingers around it and using it to pull me closer with a sly grin. "How about you? Are you exhausted, too, or...up for more?"

"Definitely up." I drop a kiss onto her mouth, but the second we make contact it's like sliding into a dizzying, euphoric high. Suddenly, everything is electric and vivid. I lose my head as I pin her to the wall. "Always up for you, baby."

Mandy tilts her head back, allowing my lips to roam her so-soft neck. I feel the heady, heavy beat of her pulse. She winds her arms around me with a moan that torques up my desire. "Tanner…"

"Bedroom?"

Before she can answer, Oliver huffs and squeals, then breaks out crying.

Mandy sighs. "Not quite yet, but hold that thought. The last few days, he's been fussier than usual, especially at night. I'm wondering if he's getting his first molars."

"Painful?"

"Apparently. Feel like pouring us some wine while I check on my little guy again?"

Not my first choice, but Oliver howls once more. Yeah, he's not happy. "I suppose the needs of my penis can wait while you see to the needs of his gums."

She laughs. "Poor baby. I'll only be a few minutes."

"Take your time. I'm not going anywhere."

She lifts onto her tiptoes and gives me a lingering kiss. "I won't be long. I promise."

Reluctantly, we part. She heads back into the bedroom with a flirty glance over her shoulder. How did I get lucky enough to persuade such a gorgeous puzzle of a woman to like me in return? I don't know, but I hope the like turns to more soon. If it does…I owe Trace. I make a mental note to buy him beers for the rest of his life.

After a quick trip to the kitchen, I pull the bottle of merlot off the quartz counter—not my first choice of drink, but Mandy likes it—and rummage around for a corkscrew. After a twist or two, followed by a soft pop, I uncork the bottle. A nearby cabinet produces a couple of wine glasses. I fill each and take them into the living room to wait. We'll talk for a bit, make sure Oliver is nice and asleep, then…it's on.

As I set the stems on the coffee table, I catch a blur of motion out of the corner of my eye. Movement. A person in dark clothing on the lanai out back, peering through the sliding door.

My heart jolts. I drag in a breath to counter its pounding as I straighten and make my way to the back of the house, trying to act as if I don't have a care in the world. No need to alert whoever's out there that I'm on to him. But once I hit the hall—out of the lurker's sight—I sprint to the bedroom and back to the closet, where Mandy leans over the crib, patting Oliver's back, trying to soothe him and still his restless kicking.

"I put some numbing gel on his gums," she says without looking up. "He should be comfortable soon."

"Mandy, listen to me. Someone is outside. A man. Where's your phone?"

She tenses, eyes flaring wide. "In my purse. In the bedroom. D-do you think it's…him?"

I pull a grim face. "Who else would be out there?"

"Any chance he's just a guy walking the beach?"

"Dressed in a ski mask and head-to-toe black while peeking in the back door?"

"Oh, my god. How could this crazy man have found me, especially so quickly?"

That's my question, too.

"Get your phone." I pull my Glock from its holster.

Mandy rushes to grab her device. "What should we do?"

"Not we. Me. I'm going out there to find him."

"What? No! It's too dangerous. Let me call the police and—"

"Don't count on them to save us. They took too long last time, and your intruder escaped. I don't know if this is the same guy, but just in case, I'll make sure he can't get away. Stay here with Oliver."

I sprint from the closet and down the hall. As I approach the living room, Glock pressed to my thigh, I relax my gait so I don't tip off the son of a bitch still peeping through the glass door. With my free hand, I lift the nearest wine glass and sip, pretending to cast a casual glance outside.

The dark shadow jerks away again.

Fuck him. I'm putting a stop to this now.

With an easy gait, I head to the kitchen. Once I'm no longer visible from the lanai door, I creep to the garage and sidestep Joe's Mustang before sneaking out to the side of the house. Pressing my back against the exterior wall, I edge toward whoever's lurking, grateful that the brisk tropical breeze and the rustling palms mask the sound of my footsteps.

When I finally reach the edge of the lanai, I spot him. He's roughly average height and average build. Good. I'm also grateful he didn't bring a mob for me to contend with. He's alone—and staring intently through the glass into the living room. If he's smart, he's wondering where the hell I went.

Then again, since he's not doing a very good job of hiding himself, he's clearly not the sharpest tool.

As I inch away from the villa, I crouch behind the lush foliage surrounding the lanai, slowly flanking him until I creep beyond his line of sight. Then, one stealthy step at a time, I sneak up behind him and press the barrel of my gun against his skull. "Hold still, motherfucker, or you'll be missing half your brain."

"D-don't shoot. Please. It's n-not what you think, I swear." His voice is a squeak, and he sounds like he's about to wet himself.

Either he's an exceptional actor or he's never committed a crime in his life, especially murder.

"Who are you?"

"Where's Amanda?"

"Shut up. You'll never touch her," I vow as I pat him down for weapons. Nothing, so I reach around him and rap on the glass door.

"What are you doing?" He trembles.

Good. He should be scared. "I'm asking the questions. Why are you after Amanda? Were you the one who tried to stab her the other night?"

Before he can answer, Mandy bustles into the living room and, wide eyed, wrenches the door open. "Oh, my god."

I shove the stalker inside, not caring when he stumbles over the threshold and falls onto the carpet on his hands and knees. "I'm guessing this is your intruder from the other night. He asked for you by name."

Mandy stares intently, as if she's trying to look through his ski mask. "What do you want? I'm calling the police."

"No!" He scrambles to his feet.

I grab his neck and squeeze, cutting off his windpipe, and press the gun to his head again. "Don't move."

He raises his hands in the air. "Amanda, please! Let me explain."

Shock and recognition cross Mandy's face. "Bruce?"

"Yes. I'm sorry." He peels off his ski mask to reveal mussed brown hair, panicked brown eyes, and a pasty face. "I didn't mean to scare you. Well, a little… I thought if you were frightened enough, you would come home and—"

"You're the one who's been terrifying me? And you broke into Nia's house with a knife?"

"Just for show. I was never going to use it."

"Oh, my god. You have stitches where I hit you with the vase?" She gazes at the angry red wound crisscrossed by dark thread.

He nods. "And a mild concussion."

"Why would you do all this?"

"Do you really have to ask? You know how I feel."

Is he serious? This was some fucked-up way of telling her he loves her?

I wedge my body between him and Mandy—and come face to face with her "nemesis." He's probably a decade younger than me, but he doesn't look as if he's spent more than ten minutes of his whole life being athletic.

Mandy glares at him around my shoulder. "You wanted to win me over so I'll…what, marry you?"

He nods earnestly. "Yes."

"And you thought scaring me would accomplish that?" She sounds as confused—and furious—as I feel.

If this guy has made half a billion dollars, he's not a complete idiot. At least in theory. "Are you fucking kidding?"

He flinches, then scowls my way. "Shut up."

"In case it's escaped you, asshole, I'm the one with the gun." I glance at Mandy over my shoulder. "Call the police."

"No! I just want to talk to her."

"Do you have his phone number?" I ask Mandy. But I already know the answer.

"Of course."

I turn to Bruce. "If she had wanted to talk to you, pal, she would have called. Instead, you tried to scare a mother and her baby and…" I glare at him. "Did you hire the angry mob, too?"

"I-I…" He stops himself, then ignores me for Mandy. "Just for show. Sweetheart, I only want to talk to you. I don't care what happened between you and Reed. I've always thought you were so beautiful that you should be my wife."

He wants her for her looks, not her heart?

Mandy shakes her head like she's still befuddled. "When did you come to Maui?"

"The day you did. My jet brought me here that same afternoon."

She looks stunned. "How did you find me?"

"Well, it was easy to guess you would go to Nia's first. You've been talking about visiting her for months."

"I mean after that."

He hesitates, wild-eyed, and my gut clenches. Whatever comes out of his mouth next is going to be a lie. I feel it in my bones.

Finally, he points my way. "From him. A couple of hours ago, he told your dad where you two were holing up so that I could persuade you to come home. By the way"—he reaches into his pocket to produce a check, then shoves it into my pocket—"here's the hundred grand he promised you. And I've got your bonus if Amanda agrees to be my wife tonight. Will you, sweetheart?" He drops to his knee. "I know this seems crazy, but that should tell you how much I want to spend my life with you."

Mandy freezes, then turns to me, gaping and angry. "You told my dad where to find me? For money?"

"No!"

I try not to be offended that she immediately believes Bruce. After all, she's known the guy most of her life. I only met her two days ago. After the way Reed treated her, it's no surprise she has deep trust issues. But damn it, I've protected her. I've listened to her. I've comforted and helped and done my best to understand her. And she believes the D-bag who skulked around like some stalker and says he wants to marry her because she's pretty?

"No, you didn't tell him? Or no, you didn't do it for the money?" She scoffs. "It doesn't matter. I trusted you. I told you everything. Oh god…"

"I didn't divulge shit to your father. He's lying." I point at Bruce. "I wouldn't betray you. You should know that."

"Should I? I want to believe you, Tanner, but how else would Bruce have known where to find us? I didn't tell anyone."

"Exactly," Bruce cuts in.

Other than a scowl, I ignore him. "Maybe he followed us. The island isn't that big, and I knew that Mustang might be a problem. Only one like it on the island, I'll bet. Or maybe…" I try to think of another plausible scenario when the truth hits me. "Your dad pinged the location of your phone and told your Romeo. Your location services were turned on until I switched them off last night."

"You snooped through my phone?"

Shit, that clearly made her mad.

"No. I opened your settings just long enough to turn off your location services. That would have been the end of it if your wannabe boyfriend hadn't started texting you. You want me to admit that I read your message string with him? Okay. Fine. I did. I was afraid he would upset you. So far, it seems like I've been proven right. I didn't mention it because it was the middle of the fucking night and you were asleep."

She presses her lips together like she's trying to decide if she believes my story. "And you couldn't tell me this morning?"

"I forgot." That's the truth.

Bruce jumps in. "Bullshit. He texted your dad a couple of hours ago and told him where I could find you. He also said how much he was looking forward to the fat, juicy paycheck and being rid of you."

"Shut up." I whirl on him. "Shut your fucking lying mouth. Here." I yank my phone from my pocket and open my texts before shoving the device in front of her. "Look through every last one of them. You won't see a single one to your father. He called the other day, but I told you about that. He texted all day, making demands and—"

"He must have deleted the text he sent back to your dad," Bruce insists.

"I didn't delete a damn thing," I growl. "We both know it."

"Even if you're telling the truth, you didn't reply to my father." Mandy looks at me like I've betrayed her. "You didn't tell him to pound sand."

Immediately, I know what she's thinking. "Not because I wanted to sell you out to him, but because I didn't think he deserved an answer simply for demanding one."

When tears fill her eyes, I know my explanation falls short.

I fucked up.

"You said you would. You promised." Her face twists, and tears fall down her cheeks. "And I believed you."

I grab her shoulders and will her to look at me. "I swear I didn't betray you, baby. If you believe nothing else, believe that. Please."

Mandy doesn't answer for a really long time. The anger bleeds from her face. "Maybe you didn't. I don't know. I really don't. But this tells me I'm not ready to trust you."

What is she saying?

"So you're going to believe him?" I gesture to Bruce. "The guy who hired a fake mob and skulked outside your door?"

"I didn't say that. But I just realized that everything is happening too fast. *You* happened too fast. I thought I was open to love again, but clearly I'm not ready to gamble the rest of my life on someone I've known for two days."

I have one last card, and if what's in my heart doesn't reach her, then I'm fucking played out. And I'm going to wind up alone— probably for good. "Do you even care that I love you?"

She crosses her arms over her chest, as if she's trying to protect herself. More tears fall. "If you really do, then you should have kept your promise. I'm sorry, but I don't think I'm ready to love you back."

"So that's it? You're going to choose Bruce and—"

"I didn't say I was choosing him."

"But you're going to," the other guy insists. "I came all the way to Hawaii and spent days here, dedicated to you and—"

"Pretending to stalk me so I'd be scared enough to fly back to New York and right into your arms? Do you think that's love?"

"No. I'm saying this all wrong. But actions speak louder, don't they? I'm prepared to slip a ring on your finger right now. I even brought it with me." He reaches into his pocket and plucks out a plush box in dark blue with a stylish HW on the front. "See? I'm serious. I know I've screwed everything up, and I'm sorry. I didn't know how else to be your hero so you'd fall for me. Let me start over, sweetheart. I promise I'll make you happy." He pries the little box open to reveal a giant oval cut diamond. "It's five carats from Harry Winston. Just say yes."

She gasps, staring at the glimmering stones. "Oh, my gosh!"

"Isn't it beautiful?"

"It is—"

"Then let me put it on your finger. Say yes."

My gut grinds with tension. Diamonds and a pretty proposal won't sway Mandy, right? "You're not seriously thinking about marrying him, are you?"

"What are you still doing here?" Bruce scowls. "She said she doesn't want you. It's time for you to leave."

I turn to Mandy. "Baby?"

"You should go. Find someone who hasn't already had her heart broken." Then she lifts her chin, and I feel the invisible wall she erects between us. "Twice."

Fuck if that doesn't hurt.

"Mandy..."

"It's Amanda now. Goodbye. I'll make sure you get compensated for your time because I keep my promises."

Ouch. "I don't want your money."

She shrugs. "I'm still going to make sure you get it. Look on the bright side. At least we know there's no one on the island out to hurt me."

I'm relieved by that but... "So you're not even going to give us a chance?"

"Tanner, I found myself falling for you too hard and too fast. But one thing I know: if you're not with me, you can't hurt me."

"I also can't comfort, love, or protect you. I can't be that man you've always wanted." Every word hurts so fucking bad. "But maybe that's all right since you've decided not to be the brave, ballsy woman I know you can be. Oh, and in case you thought I was nothing but a mercenary prick"—I yank out the check Bruce stuffed in my pocket and tear it until it's confetti—"I'm not. Goodbye."

Chapter Eleven

The next day, I'm awakened just like I was three days ago—by my cell phone chiming a lousy breakup song I've assigned as my ex's ringtone. But this time it's not Bon Jovi warning me that Ellie is up in my business. Gwen Stefani voicing No Doubt's "Don't Speak" tells me it's Mandy calling.

Excuse me, Amanda.

She told me to take a hike less than twelve hours ago, and I assigned her that tune because it honestly felt like she didn't want to hear me. Or couldn't. Not a single word I said. She listened to her fear, not to the man who wanted to love her for life. And I lost. So what does she want now that we're over?

I almost don't answer until I hear a groan on the other side of the small apartment. "Are you going to get that or just let it wake me up again?"

Shit. It's Joe. I banged on his door when I left the villa and asked to crash on his sofa for the night. He must have seen how messed up I was. If my mood didn't tell him, the bottle in my fist—which I proceeded to drain—surely clued him in.

"Sorry." I sit up and reach for my phone to silence it. And I instantly regret it. My head hurts like a bitch.

"Answer it already. Whoever that is has called three times in ten minutes."

She has? Apparently, and I didn't hear it.

"All right. Sorry. Go back to sleep." I creep from the sofa, grateful I'm wearing my shorts, then head out to the balcony, phone in hand, squinting against the morning light. As soon as I shut the door behind me, I answer the call. "Are you in danger?"

"N-no. Tanner, I—"

"Are you all right?"

"Physically, yes, but—"

"Then we don't have anything else to say. You made yourself pretty clear last night."

"Actually, I didn't," she says softly. "Would you come by the villa this morning? Please."

I tense. My head pounds unmercifully. I don't dare get my hopes up. "Why?"

"I just want to talk. Ten minutes. I won't keep you longer than that."

On the one hand, I don't want to give her the opportunity to hurt me again. I told her I loved her and I meant it. Despite everything between us, she didn't choose me. Hell, she didn't even bat an eye when I said the words. On the other hand...I want to see her so fucking badly, even if it's going to hurt like hell. I doubt she'll realize she's made a mistake, but that doesn't change how greedy I am to lay eyes on her.

"Looking to rip my heart out again?"

"That's not it at all. I promise."

God, I feel like such a sucker. "Fine. I'll be there in thirty."

"Thank you." She sounds so earnest. "Really. You won't regret it."

I already do, but for some fucking reason I still love her too much to refuse. I don't say anything, though. I just hang up and stride back into the apartment.

Joe is standing there, waiting in a ratty blue terrycloth bathrobe. "You less miserable now?"

I rub at my aching forehead, but nothing is putting a dent in this hangover. "Not really."

"That Amanda?"

How much did I tell him last night? Honestly, I don't remember a lot beyond twisting the cap off my vodka and snarling that I wanted some time alone. "Yeah. She wants to 'talk,' whatever that means. Sorry if I was an asshole last night."

"You weren't an asshole. You were broken-hearted. I don't know this girl at all, but I know you love her."

"It doesn't matter if it's not reciprocated."

"Are you sure it isn't?" he challenges. "Cam's mother and I..."

"Split a long time ago." Camden told me the stories. He was in seventh grade, and his dad left one night. Filed for divorce the next day.

"Because I was an idiot. One of my buddies intimated my wife was having a fling with the contractor remodeling our kitchen. He was there with her all day, alone a lot of the time. Whenever I'd come home, they'd be so deep in conversation they'd barely notice me. Sex had gone to hell. So I was convinced my buddy was right." He scoffs bitterly. "Turns out, my buddy just wanted my wife for himself. Two years after our divorce, he married her."

"You and Teddy were friends?" I can't even picture that.

"From high school until the day I found out he was banging Brenda." He shakes his head. "The whole breakup was my fault. I let my pride do my talking, not my heart. And I spent the rest of my fucking life in misery. Don't repeat my mistake. Because the worst day of my life was getting a letter from Brenda just before she died of breast cancer telling me that she'd never once cheated on me and she'd never stopped loving me. I realized I'd pissed away fifteen years we could have had together."

That really sucks. "I'm sorry. But I'm not here because I had too much pride. I'm here because Amanda told me to leave."

"Sure, but she's asked you to come back to talk. Don't let your pride stand in your way."

"It's not. I said I'd be there."

"You'll go, sure." He peers at me, and I see a lifetime of sadness on his face. He'd give anything for a do-over that's never coming. "But will you really listen?"

It's a fair question. I honestly don't know the answer. Did I agree to go through the motions for closure? Pretty much. Would the conversation be any different if I resolved not to go in with a chip on my shoulder?

"I'll do my best."

He studies me, then finally nods. "I've spent the last twenty years alone because I was a dumb ass. And I've lived with so much regret... Do yourself a favor. If she wants to work it out, try. Or you'll be like me—almost sixty, alone, and unable to commit to anyone because I buried my heart with the woman I love the day she died five years ago."

Fuck. That's rough. "All right. I'll listen."

He claps me on the shoulder. It makes my pounding head feel like it's about to burst. "Good. Cam's been lucky to have you as a friend. Now go take a shower. You look like shit. I'll make coffee."

I probably do look like shit. "Thanks. Got some ibuprofen?"

"Bathroom cabinet."

"I appreciate it." I also respect the hell out of him. He poured out his heart and gave me wisdom when he could have said nothing and let me fuck this up alone. "And I'll make the best of my situation with Amanda."

The pain tablets help soothe my head, along with a glass of water, a scalding shower, and a black coffee for the road. At the door, I wave to Joe then plop into his Mustang and head back to the villa.

Does Amanda just want to explain her rationale? Does she want to say she's sorry for being unable to trust me—or anyone—after what Barclay pulled on her? Probably some combination of both. Sure, it's possible she loves me, too, and wants to spend her life with me. I'd love that...but I'm not counting on it.

Other than Tuesday morning commuters, the drive is too silent. I'm too alone with my thoughts and the pictures dive-bombing my brain of Amanda and everything that went south between us last night.

I turn on the radio. The country station she found during our last drive fills my classic ride. I don't know what song is playing. I don't know who the hell sings it. But after a few notes I'm sucked in. And I swear whoever wrote this song is a fucking mind reader.

Just like the guy singing, I know I'll be a mess the second Amanda walks into the room because it happens every time. It's nothing new, but the way my heart aches and throbs, I expect it will be damn hard to hold my shit together.

Because whenever Amanda looks at me with those eyes, I'm speechless. If she wasn't sure, after this morning she'll have no doubt she's my weakness. It started even before she said hello, and I'm convinced I'll feel this way until the day I die.

When the vocalist croons again that he's speechless, I turn the radio off. I'd rather deal with silence than be bombarded by maudlin shit that tugs at my heart.

When I pull up to the villa, I see a sleek gray Mercedes parked in front. Whose fucking car is that? Is Bruce here? Did he spend the night? Did she really go from my arms to his? Did she drag me here to tell me she's decided to marry him after all?

I slam the 'Stang's door, then dry my suddenly sweaty palms on my shorts as I head up the walkway to the villa's front door and knock.

But it isn't Amanda who answers. Instead, I'm greeted by a tall, thirtyish blond guy with blue eyes, a hundred-dollar dress shirt, and a smooth demeanor.

I rear back. Who's this guy?

"You Tanner?" he asks.

"Yeah." I'm suspicious—until I look at his eyes. They're so much like Amanda's. "Stephen?"

"Come in." He steps back to admit me. "My sister thought it was time we have a family meeting."

So why the hell am I here?

"Coffee?" He leads me toward the kitchen.

I didn't finish mine in the car, and my head is still nagging at me. "That would be great."

He peers my way. "Your eyes are bloodshot, and you're squinting like the overhead light hurts your head. Hungover?"

Fuck, this bastard is perceptive. "A little."

"Whiskey?"

"Vodka."

"Toasting my sister, I'm presume?"

This is the weirdest conversation. I didn't come here to meet her brother...though I have to wonder why he's yapping at me now. "Where is she?"

"Changing Oliver and getting dressed. Hey, Dad..."

I turn to find an older version of Stephen entering the room. His shoulders have begun to round with age. His slicked-back hair is more than a little silver. He smiles my way and sticks out his hand. "Mr. Kirk, we finally meet."

I'm just not sure why.

Reluctantly, I shake his hand in return. "Mr. Lund."

"Douglas," he corrects.

Stephen offers me a fresh mug. "Cream? Sugar?"

"Black."

He takes a sip of his own brew with a sigh. "A man after my own heart."

"Forgive me, but I thought I was here to talk to Amanda. If you two brought me here to threaten, bribe, or bully me into getting the hell out of her life, you can stop. She already tossed me out, and I left. Mission accomplished."

"That's not why she asked you to come," Lund Senior assures. "I want to apologize for busting in like a bull in a china shop and to thank you."

Am I hearing this right? "For what?"

"Being the kind of man my daughter needs. I misjudged you."

"I don't understand."

"Amanda called us here and reamed us out for interfering. Then she explained what you did for her, how you put her first...and I realized I'd judged you wrong. I feared you had the same motives as Barclay."

It takes me a minute to connect the dots. "You thought I would use my position of power as her protector to seduce her because I wanted a piece of ass."

Stephen laughs, and Lund Senior has the good grace to look chastened. "Not the words I would have chosen—"

"Only because he's more blunt," Amanda's brother puts in.

The older man concedes with a nod. "But that was my fear, yes."

I understand a man wanting to protect his daughter, but does he know her at all? "She's not weak. She's not a pushover. And she's definitely not easy."

At least I never thought she was. But if she's engaged to Bruce now...

"I'm beginning to grasp that. Last night, she called and unloaded more than a few choice words on me. I happened to be in San Francisco on business, so when she demanded I... What was it she said?" He looks Stephen's way.

"To stop treating her like a kid, get your ass out to Maui, and listen for once, damn it."

Lund Senior nods. "Yeah. That sums it up. So I hopped on a red-eye, and we've spent the last few hours talking. We know everything about Barclay now. The whole truth. I had no idea..."

Really? "So you know she was just a child when—"

"Yeah." And the truth is clearly killing him. "I feel so guilty that I never saw it."

"I had my suspicions," Stephen admits. "I should have done more. I'll have to live with that regret. But after she gave us both a tongue lashing, she called you over so we could apologize to you for assuming the worst, butting in, and being pains in your ass."

"Precisely," Amanda's father seconds. "I hope there are no hard feelings."

It's damn hard not to have them. "Bruce wasn't the answer, and you shouldn't have told him where to find Amanda last night."

"I know. I just wanted to protect my daughter from more heartache, and I knew he'd never hurt her."

He'd never make her happy, either.

"She's perfectly capable of managing her own life." And dishing out heartache in return.

I ought to know.

"We're, um…figuring that out." Stephen laughs at himself.

I wish I had a sense of humor now. But Amanda still hasn't appeared. Because she didn't really want to see me? Her family apologizing is all well and good, but who gives a shit if she and I have no future?

"We are," Lund Senior assures me. "So I hope you'll accept our sincere apologies. I also wanted to give you this."

When he thrusts an envelope in my hands, I open it to find a check for ten grand. "What's this?"

"The money Amanda owes you, plus expenses…and a bonus for putting up with us."

For him, it's chump change. And I'm not a chump. I need the money, but not enough to compromise my ethics.

"No thanks." I push the envelope back at him. "I appreciate the apology, but I don't need it. I won't take your money, either. I came to talk to Amanda, but if she didn't ask me here to talk to me herself, I've got nothing left to say."

With a curt nod, I turn away. I fucking wanted that money when Amanda hired me. I wanted that apology after her family tried to bully me.

Now I just want Amanda.

Sure, I could march to the back of the house and demand that she talk to me. But it would be pointless. She has to want to meet me halfway. And if she doesn't… Well, forcing her would accomplish nothing. Best to tuck away the memory of our time together and walk away like a man.

Footsteps take me closer to the door. With every second, my dread grows. I wanted to see Amanda one last time. I didn't even get that. I'm leaving empty-handed, poorer, and broken fucking hearted.

The first two I can deal with. The last… I have no idea how I'll get over. Even losing Ellie didn't hurt this much.

Then I hear the voice that first gripped me, even before I saw the face that went with it. And just like the earlier song said, it leaves me tongue-tied and speechless. "Tanner, wait!"

* * * *

Amanda

After settling Oliver in my brother's capable arms, I wring my hands and stare at the back of Tanner's big, broad shoulders, willing him to face me.

Slowly, he pivots. His dark eyes are stark and pain-filled. Seeing him is a body blow. I press my hand to my chest. It feels like I've stopped breathing. Like the world has stopped turning.

How am I going to reach him before he walks out the door for good?

"I'm sorry," I blurt and approach him slowly.

The raw tangle of anger and pain on his face nearly kills me. I did this. He tried to help me when I needed it. He protected me when I felt threatened. He listened when I needed understanding. And he loved me when I started to fall.

I repaid him with a knee-jerk, courtesy of my fear and mistrust. I didn't listen to his side of the story before I sent him away. I owe him at least that—and so much more.

"For what?"

He tries to look impassive, but I see through his expression. He hasn't slept much and he's hurting. I feel horrible.

"Last night. Overreacting." I remember the rest of my family is standing in the middle of the kitchen, watching us. "Would you come with me? Like I said, ten minutes. Please."

Tanner hesitates, his gaze flicking over the other men in my life before settling on me again. "All right. Ten minutes."

He's already hedging his bets, and I don't blame him.

As he heads back in my direction, I ease closer. Our fingers brush. As I lead him to the sliding glass door at the back of the villa, I ache to tuck my hand in his, but I have so much to say before I have any right to touch him. And I respect that because I know too much about what it's like to be touched by someone who shouldn't.

Like a gentleman, he opens the door and leads me out. His guiding hand at the small of my back makes me tingle. Then it's gone in a flash, and I feel alone again.

Tanner shuts the door, then glances at his watch as if he's taking note of the time before he crosses his arms over his chest. "What?"

He's not hostile...but he's not friendly. I don't blame him. He's just coming out of a divorce. I'm probably the first person he opened his heart to since his ex-wife. And I treated him horribly.

"I wish I had a do-over on last night. Everything happened so fast, and I admit I was terrified of being hurt again."

"I would never have hurt you on purpose, but you were too afraid to even listen."

He's not wrong. I swallow, wishing again that I could touch him. "The minute you were gone, I realized that I was way more afraid of being without you than I am of being hurt by you."

"I don't know if I can believe that. I told you I love you—"

"And I love you, too. I'm sure everyone will think we're crazy. A week ago, I had no idea you even existed. Now I can't imagine living without you."

His posture relaxes. His arms drop from his chest. "What are you saying?"

Here's my moment. I drag in a deep breath and go for broke. "I want you. With me. Near me. Protecting me—"

"If I stay, it's because I'm doing more than protecting you."

"Yes!" I dare to step closer, but I have to clench my fists to stop myself from touching him. "I want you to love me, too. Now. Today. Forever. I don't know if that makes sense or if you're ready—"

"Fuck, Mandy." He grips my shoulders and hauls me closer, wrapping that possessive palm around my nape and sliding my mouth inches under his. "Are you sure?"

"Very." Tears sting my eyes.

"I think I've known from the minute I laid eyes on you that I wanted to love you forever. You're not afraid anymore?"

"I am. I can't lie, but I won't give in to fear. I'm determined to put the past behind me." I caress his face. "I want to be with you. I don't know what that means yet or what that looks like but—"

"We'll figure it out together."

My lips tremble as I smile. "I wouldn't want it any other way. You definitely staying on Maui?"

He hesitates. "I thought about that some last night. I like it here. I'm ready to start over and make a new life. Maui seems like a good place. I know there are a lot of good people."

I nod. "I have a new job. You have a new range to open…"

"Neither of us have a place to live." His fingers tighten around me. "You thinking we should find one together?"

My smile widens. "Why wouldn't I live with the man I love?"

Finally, an answering grin slides up his face. "You should. So…we'll find a place."

"Soon, yeah." I look into his dark eyes. There's nowhere I feel happier or safer. "I can't wait."

He drags me against him. "Same, baby."

Then Tanner dips his head and slides a slow, solemn kiss across my lips. I feel the weight of it. The seriousness. It's a solemn vow, so I answer in turn, holding nothing back. This time when my heart lurches like it wants to be closer to him, I know he'll be there for me. And I'm right. He holds me tight and barges into my mouth, like the dam of his restraint broke. The kiss suddenly turns relentless and passionate. Eternal.

"I love you," he pants.

"I love you, too. I'm sorry I ever made you doubt that. I won't do that again."

He tucks a strand of hair behind my ear. "I'm going to marry you someday."

My smile turns up to something even more uncontained. "Yeah? Are you asking?"

His expression turns wry. "I have to officially be divorced first, but…once that's done, I just might."

Given the possessive way he's holding me, I know he will. One step at a time. One day at a time. We'll find our forever.

"I'd like that. What should we do now?"

His hand travels my spine, burning a path down my body until he cups my hip and presses me against his hardness. "How long are your dad and your brother staying?"

"I can tell them to get lost anytime. But you know Oliver and I come as a package deal."

"Absolutely. I have a feeling your little guy will keep our lives interesting."

"Along with other children? You want them, right?"

"Hell, yeah. The sooner the better."

Me, too. And I hate this, but I have to ask. "Everything really has happened so fast. Are you sure?"

"Damn straight. Are you?"

"For the first time in my life, I know I'm exactly where and who I belong with."

"Mandy…" He brings me close and kisses me again, slowly, heatedly, thoroughly.

Reluctantly, I break away. "That's it. I need you. I'm telling my family to leave. Oliver should be down for a nap in the next thirty minutes."

"Good. Then we'll get on with the rest of our lives. What do you say?"

"Yes. You're my forever. I know that in my heart now."

"I feel it too, baby. Let's get started."

Then he takes my hand and leads me inside, so we can start our future together.

<<< >>>

The End

* * * *

Also from 1001 Dark Nights and Shayla Black, discover More Than Pleasure You, Dirty Wicked, Forever Wicked and Pure Wicked.

Sign up for the 1001 Dark Nights Newsletter
and be entered to win a Tiffany Key necklace.

There's a contest every month!

Go to www.1001DarkNights.com to subscribe.

**As a bonus, all subscribers can download
FIVE FREE exclusive books!**

Discover 1001 Dark Nights Collection Seven

THE BISHOP by Skye Warren
A Tanglewood Novella

TAKEN WITH YOU by Carrie Ann Ryan
A Fractured Connections Novella

DRAGON LOST by Donna Grant
A Dark Kings Novella

SEXY LOVE by Carly Phillips
A Sexy Series Novella

PROVOKE by Rachel Van Dyken
A Seaside Pictures Novella

RAFE by Sawyer Bennett
An Arizona Vengeance Novella

THE NAUGHTY PRINCESS by Claire Contreras
A Sexy Royals Novella

THE GRAVEYARD SHIFT by Darynda Jones
A Charley Davidson Novella

CHARMED by Lexi Blake
A Masters and Mercenaries Novella

SACRIFICE OF DARKNESS by Alexandra Ivy
A Guardians of Eternity Novella

THE QUEEN by Jen Armentrout
A Wicked Novella

BEGIN AGAIN by Jennifer Probst
A Stay Novella

VIXEN by Rebecca Zanetti
A Dark Protectors/Rebels Novella

SLASH by Laurelin Paige
A Slay Series Novella

THE DEAD HEAT OF SUMMER by Heather Graham
A Krewe of Hunters Novella

WILD FIRE by Kristen Ashley
A Chaos Novella

MORE THAN PROTECT YOU by Shayla Black
A More Than Words Novella

LOVE SONG by Kylie Scott
A Stage Dive Novella

CHERISH ME by J. Kenner
A Stark Ever After Novella

SHINE WITH ME by Kristen Proby
A With Me in Seattle Novella

And new from Blue Box Press:

TEASE ME by J. Kenner
A Stark International Novel

FROM BLOOD AND ASH by Jennifer L. Armentrout
A Blood and Ash Novel

QUEEN MOVE by Kennedy Ryan

THE HOUSE OF LONG AGO by Steve Berry and MJ Rose
A Cassiopeia Vitt Adventure

THE BUTTERFLY ROOM by Lucinda Riley

A KINGDOM OF FLESH AND FIRE by Jennifer L. Armentrout
A Blood and Ash Novel

Discover More Shayla Black

More Than Pleasure You
A More Than Words Novella

Can I convince her our hot but temporary engagement should last forever?

I'm Stephen Lund, confirmed bachelor…and son of a successful billionaire whose sins I can't forget—or forgive. Though he insisted I get over his transgressions, I can't. So I put space between us with a temporary getaway to Maui. My rental's sexy caretaker, Skye Ingram, is a beautiful distraction. Yeah, it's a terrible time to start a fling, but I can't help wanting to give her every bit of pleasure she's willing to take.

When Skye needs a date to her ex-boyfriend's wedding, I'm game to play her pretend fiancé. The jerk should see what he passed up…and that I'm holding her now. But our pretend engagement begins to feel real. Our passion certainly is. So are the consequences. When I'm confronted with the reality that our lives are now irrevocably entwined, I have to choose between leaving Skye to return to the life—and wealth—I've always known or abandoning everything familiar to start over with the woman who awakened my heart.

* * * *

Dirty Wicked
A Wicked Lovers Novella

After being framed for a crime he didn't commit, former private eye Nick Navarro has nothing but revenge on his mind—until a woman from his past returns to beg for his help.

Beautiful widow Sasha Porter has been hunted by his enemies. Desperate, she offers him anything to keep her young daughter safe, even agreeing to become his mistress. The last thing either of them want are emotional entanglements but as they entrap the ruthless politician who arranged Nick's downfall and passion sizzles between them, danger closes in.

Will he choose love over vengeance before it's too late?

Pure Wicked
A Wicked Lovers Novella

During his decade as an international pop star, Jesse McCall has lived every day in the fast lane. A committed hedonist reveling in amazing highs, globetrotting, and nameless encounters, he refuses to think about his loneliness or empty future. Then tragedy strikes.

Shocked and grieving, he sheds his identity and walks away, searching for peace. Instead, he finds Bristol Reese, a no-nonsense beauty scraping to keep her business afloat while struggling with her own demons. He's intent on seducing her, but other than a pleasure-filled night, she's not interested in a player, especially after her boyfriend recently proposed to her sister. In order to claim Bristol, Jesse has to prove he's not the kind of man he's always been. But when she learns his identity and his past comes back to haunt him, how will he convince her that he's a changed man who wants nothing more than to make her his forever?

Forever Wicked
A Wicked Lovers Novella

They had nothing in common but a desperate passion…

Billionaire Jason Denning lived life fast and hard in a world where anything could be bought and sold, even affection. But all that changed when he met "Greta," a beautiful stranger ready to explore her hidden desires. From a blue collar family, Gia Angelotti wore a badge, fought for right—and opened herself utterly to love him. Blindsided and falling hard, Jason does the first impulsive thing of his life and hustles her to the altar.

Until a second chance proved that forever could be theirs.

Then tragedy ripped Jason's new bride from his arms and out of his life. When he finds Gia again, he gives her a choice: spend the three weeks before their first anniversary with him or forfeit the money she receives from their marriage. Reluctantly, she agrees to once again put herself at his mercy and return to his bed. But having her right where he wants her is dangerous for Jason's peace of mind. No matter how hard he tries, he finds himself falling for her again. Will he learn to trust that their love is real before Gia leaves again for good?

More Than Dare You
More Than Words, Book 6
By Shayla Black
Now Available

Want to know more about Trace and Masey, shown in More Than Protect You? Read on…

I dared her to spend a hot, no-strings night with me. Now I'm determined to keep her forever.

I'm Trace Weston, recently reformed womanizer. In the blink of an eye, I went from busy bachelor to full-time single dad. My life was already complicated before my sister-in-law asked me to show off my bedroom skills to her bestie, who's wanting to experience real pleasure now that her one-and-only long-term relationship is over. Gorgeous Masey Garrett isn't my "usual." She's shy, sassy, driven, and incredibly kind. Suddenly I'm falling fast…but she's only mine for a night.

What's a former player to do? Change the rules.

Now she's under my roof night after night, letting me into her body and her life. Her heart? Not so much. She loves my newborn son. Me? I can't tell. I'm pulling out all the stops to win her over, but she's not taking me seriously. Other than passion, how can I reach her? Every attempt only pulls me deeper under her spell. Sure, I could drop an <I>L<\I> bomb…except that once imploded my heart. But when her past collides with my desired future, can I risk everything and dare Masey to stay with me forever?

Excerpt:

"I'm the girl desperate enough to ask her best friend if she knew a guy willing to spend tonight with me so I could experience sex without my ex. You can't actually be interested in me beyond the fact I'm an easy lay."

I don't know whether I should wring Thom's neck or hers. "You're going to learn to stop selling yourself short, even if I have to spend all night kissing the bad habit out of you…"

She swallows. "Why?"

Because we have chemistry for days, honey. But I'm not going to waste the breath looking for the right words to convince her I think she's sexy as fuck when I've got a better way. I crook my finger at her. "Come closer and let me demonstrate." When she hesitates, I grin her way. "I dare you."

Masey draws in a sharp, shallow breath and holds it as she searches my face. Her pulse pounds. A tremor shudders through her. She licks her lips.

I have the distinct impression she's nervous…but tempted. The attraction is getting to her, wearing down her hesitation. Or maybe she's considering giving in because the alternative is merely the status quo. Whatever. Knowing she's nearly in the palm of my hand is a fucking turn-on.

My stare drops to her mouth. It was made for kissing. For sex. Everything about it tempts me. She's still wearing the remnants of a rosy gloss that accentuates the pout of her full lips. I want to kiss them, feel them glide across my skin, see them wrap around my cock.

"You dare me?" She raises an arched brow.

I drag in a breath to cool the lust burning my veins. "Yeah."

About Shayla Black

Shayla Black is the *New York Times* and *USA Today* bestselling author of roughly eighty novels. For twenty years, she's written contemporary, erotic, paranormal, and historical romances via traditional, independent, foreign, and audio publishers. Her books have sold millions of copies and been published in a dozen languages.

Raised an only child, Shayla occupied herself with lots of daydreaming, much to the chagrin of her teachers. In college, she found her love for reading and realized that she could have a career publishing the stories spinning in her imagination. Though she graduated with a degree in Marketing/Advertising and embarked on a stint in corporate America to pay the bills, she abandoned all that to be with her characters full-time.

Shayla currently lives in North Texas with her wonderfully supportive husband and daughter, as well as two spoiled tabbies. In her "free" time, she enjoys reality TV, reading, and listening to an eclectic blend of music.

Connect with me via the links below!

Text Alerts
To receive sale and new release alerts to your phone, text SHAYLA to 24587.
Website http://shaylablack.com
Reading order, Book Boyfriend sorter, FAQs, excerpts, audio clips, and more!
VIP Reader Newsletter http://shayla.link/nwsltr
Exclusive content, new release alerts, cover reveals, free books!
Facebook Book Beauties Chat Group
    http://shayla.link/FBChat
Interact with me! Wine Wednesday LIVE video weekly. Fun, community, and chatter.
Facebook Author Page http://shayla.link/FBPage
News, teasers, announcements, weekly romance release lists...
BookBub http://shayla.link/BookBub

Learn about my sales and new releases!
Instagram https://instagram.com/ShaylaBlack/
See what I'm up to in pictures!
Goodreads http://shayla.link/goodreads
Keep track of your reads and mark my next book TBR so you don't forget!
Pinterest http://shayla.link/Pinterest
Juicy teasers and other fun about your fave Shayla Black books!
YouTube http://shayla.link/youtube
Book trailers, videos, and more coming…

If you enjoy this book, please review/recommend it. That means the world to me!

Discover 1001 Dark Nights

COLLECTION THREE
HIDDEN INK by Carrie Ann Ryan
BLOOD ON THE BAYOU by Heather Graham
SEARCHING FOR MINE by Jennifer Probst
DANCE OF DESIRE by Christopher Rice
ROUGH RHYTHM by Tessa Bailey
DEVOTED by Lexi Blake
Z by Larissa Ione
FALLING UNDER YOU by Laurelin Paige
EASY FOR KEEPS by Kristen Proby
UNCHAINED by Elisabeth Naughton
HARD TO SERVE by Laura Kaye
DRAGON FEVER by Donna Grant
KAYDEN/SIMON by Alexandra Ivy/Laura Wright
STRUNG UP by Lorelei James
MIDNIGHT UNTAMED by Lara Adrian
TRICKED by Rebecca Zanetti
DIRTY WICKED by Shayla Black
THE ONLY ONE by Lauren Blakely
SWEET SURRENDER by Liliana Hart

COLLECTION FOUR
ROCK CHICK REAWAKENING by Kristen Ashley
ADORING INK by Carrie Ann Ryan
SWEET RIVALRY by K. Bromberg
SHADE'S LADY by Joanna Wylde
RAZR by Larissa Ione
ARRANGED by Lexi Blake
TANGLED by Rebecca Zanetti
HOLD ME by J. Kenner
SOMEHOW, SOME WAY by Jennifer Probst
TOO CLOSE TO CALL by Tessa Bailey
HUNTED by Elisabeth Naughton
EYES ON YOU by Laura Kaye
BLADE by Alexandra Ivy/Laura Wright
DRAGON BURN by Donna Grant
TRIPPED OUT by Lorelei James
STUD FINDER by Lauren Blakely
MIDNIGHT UNLEASHED by Lara Adrian
HALLOW BE THE HAUNT by Heather Graham

DIRTY FILTHY FIX by Laurelin Paige
THE BED MATE by Kendall Ryan
NIGHT GAMES by CD Reiss
NO RESERVATIONS by Kristen Proby
DAWN OF SURRENDER by Liliana Hart

COLLECTION FIVE
BLAZE ERUPTING by Rebecca Zanetti
ROUGH RIDE by Kristen Ashley
HAWKYN by Larissa Ione
RIDE DIRTY by Laura Kaye
ROME'S CHANCE by Joanna Wylde
THE MARRIAGE ARRANGEMENT by Jennifer Probst
SURRENDER by Elisabeth Naughton
INKED NIGHTS by Carrie Ann Ryan
ENVY by Rachel Van Dyken
PROTECTED by Lexi Blake
THE PRINCE by Jennifer L. Armentrout
PLEASE ME by J. Kenner
WOUND TIGHT by Lorelei James
STRONG by Kylie Scott
DRAGON NIGHT by Donna Grant
TEMPTING BROOKE by Kristen Proby
HAUNTED BE THE HOLIDAYS by Heather Graham
CONTROL by K. Bromberg
HUNKY HEARTBREAKER by Kendall Ryan
THE DARKEST CAPTIVE by Gena Showalter

COLLECTION SIX
DRAGON CLAIMED by Donna Grant
ASHES TO INK by Carrie Ann Ryan
ENSNARED by Elisabeth Naughton
EVERMORE by Corinne Michaels
VENGEANCE by Rebecca Zanetti
ELI'S TRIUMPH by Joanna Wylde
CIPHER by Larissa Ione
RESCUING MACIE by Susan Stoker
ENCHANTED by Lexi Blake
TAKE THE BRIDE by Carly Phillips
INDULGE ME by J. Kenner

THE KING by Jennifer L. Armentrout
QUIET MAN by Kristen Ashley
ABANDON by Rachel Van Dyken
THE OPEN DOOR by Laurelin Paige
CLOSER by Kylie Scott
SOMETHING JUST LIKE THIS by Jennifer Probst
BLOOD NIGHT by Heather Graham
TWIST OF FATE by Jill Shalvis
MORE THAN PLEASURE YOU by Shayla Black
WONDER WITH ME by Kristen Proby
THE DARKEST ASSASSIN by Gena Showalter

Discover Blue Box Press

TAME ME by J. Kenner
TEMPT ME by J. Kenner
DAMIEN by J. Kenner
TEASE ME by J. Kenner
REAPER by Larissa Ione
THE SURRENDER GATE by Christopher Rice
SERVICING THE TARGET by Cherise Sinclair
THE LAKE OF LEARNING by Steve Berry and MJ Rose
THE MUSEUM OF MYSTERIES by Steve Berry and MJ Rose

On Behalf of 1001 Dark Nights,

Liz Berry, M.J. Rose, and Jillian Stein would like to thank ~

Steve Berry
Doug Scofield
Benjamin Stein
Kim Guidroz
Social Butterfly PR
Ashley Wells
Asha Hossain
Chris Graham
Chelle Olson
Kasi Alexander
Jessica Johns
Dylan Stockton
Richard Blake
and Simon Lipskar